Dead Drop

I0663724

Does the past ever really leave us? Not in Amy Lynch's world.

What starts out to be a well-deserved vacation for Amy – volunteering at an archaeological dig on the outskirts of Paris – turns ugly when the head archaeologist is found dead at the dig-site. A recently-uncovered relic from World War II threatens to expose treachery and betrayal from the time of the German Occupation. It endangers the life of anybody bold enough to delve into its significance.

New England Casualty and Indemnity, the insurance company where Amy works as a claims investigator, is insuring the dig. Amy's world turns upside-down as she reverts from vacation mode to conduct a full-blown investigation. She meets with obstacles, resistance and threats to her own safety – as well as an adorable French detective – in her quest to unmask a traitor.

"Norton has created an engaging protagonist in Amy, who is bright, brave, and tenacious. The tale features a small cast of characters, as many players disappear shortly after being introduced, so Amy has to carry the narrative load. Fortunately, she's up to the challenge; readers should quickly get involved in what happens to the feisty, heady heroine. With a neat twist in her fast-paced narrative, the author illustrates how events from 80 years in the past can affect people in the present, even Amy herself. Norton seamlessly blends history and mystery into a spellbinding thriller. This sequel accomplishes the unlikely feat of making an insurance investigator enthralling."

—Kirkus Reviews

Deep Secrets

Dead men tell no tales. Is that why Tom Griffin is lying near death in a Cape Cod hospital? Because of what he could reveal about Waltower—a top secret government project underway at Woods Hole Oceanographic Institute?

That's what Amy Lynch aims to learn. As an investigator for New England Casualty and Indemnity, Amy's job is to look into the supposed accident that put Tom into a coma. Amy has a personal stake as well. Tom Griffin is an old friend. Her first love. She struggles to keep her emotions in check as she seeks to discover what really happened to Tom. And why.

Amy fights her way through the sand-bagging she receives from WHOI. They say the project is need-to-know. Well, Amy needs to know. And the clearer the situation becomes to her, the greater the threat to her safety.

Will she uncover the truth in time to save herself from the same fate as Tom?

"If you love reading solid mysteries with a heroine you can identify with, then look no further than novelist P.K. Norton. Deep Secrets is her latest installment featuring intrepid insurance investigator Amy Lynch. Amy is no ordinary sleuth and the mystery set in and around Cape Cod will keep you guessing to the end!"

—Jordan Rich
WBZ iHeart Radio

"Norton draws on her experience working in the insurance industry to good effect in this latest series outing ... [she] manages to make insurance-related details as compelling as evidence collection in a conventional murder mystery. The plot is well-paced ... the characters are well-drawn. An entertaining, well-plotted mystery that offers good characterization and unexpected twists and turns."

—Kirkus Reviews

ALSO BY P.K. NORTON

Deadly Diamonds

Are diamonds really a girl's best friend? Are they actually forever? And what is causing the sudden epidemic of diamond jewelry disappearing from households across Massachusetts? Insurance investigator Amy Lynch sets out to answer this question when theft claims at New England Casualty and Indemnity take an alarming upturn. What she discovers about the NEC&I agents who insure these diamonds takes her down a dark and disturbing road – a road from which she almost fails to return.

Norton's latest installment in her Amy Lynch Investigation series features accessible prose and likable characters, and it benefits from the fact that mysteries set in the insurance industry are relatively rare. The story opens strongly, with a stealth murder from the perspective of the killer, and Norton flows easily from that point ... A novel with appealing characters and a good setup

—Kirkus Reviews

PK Norton is back with another finely cut mystery! It's Amy Lynch at her best, investigating a rash of diamond robberies...Murder is in the air and Amy is in a race to solve the crime before she, too, becomes a victim. One cannot help but admire Amy as we stay up late reading to find out how she will go about cracking another beguiling case. She is resourceful, smart and just the kind of woman all of us want to root for.

—Jordan Rich,
WBZ Boston, iHeart media

Sweet Dreams, Sweet Death

Everybody loves Chef Garcia's key lime coconut petit fours. Some even say they're to die for. When four guests die at a wedding at the Beaux Rêves Hotel, the famous petit fours are blamed.

Insurance investigator Amy Lynch flies to Key West to prepare for a wrongful death suit. Her investigation is beset with problems. Hotel management pushes for a quick settlement regardless of fault. Local police call it a tragic accident. Potential witnesses are missing, deceased, or unhelpful. Amy fends off pressures from all sides and encounters death everywhere. The health inspector dies in an accident; the local reporter turns up drowned; a homeless woman Amy befriends is found dead. And deceased wildlife crosses her path more than once.

As she forges on in the face of these obstacles, Amy wonders if Key West is the tropical paradise of the travel brochures or a petri dish of death.

"Norton weaves realistic professional procedure and unexpected emotional jolts into the otherwise erotic flavor of Key West, creating a debut that will seriously contend for all the 'Best First' awards."

—Author Jeremiah Healy

"An impressively crafted and unfailingly entertaining novel by a master of the genre, Sweet Dreams, Sweet Death by P.K. Norton is the first volume in what promises to be a simply outstanding new series starring Amy Lynch, female investigator."

—James A. Cox
Editor-in-Chief, Midwest Book Review

Direct Elimination

There is no such thing as a coincidence. Or is there? Are random occurrences which take place at the same time, or in the same location, totally unrelated events? Or do they converge in time and space in order to right a wrong or put the universe back on track?

In other words, is there a connection between the dead fencer found by firefighters in Andy Yesley's cellar and the 20-year-old baby's skeleton also discovered there?

This is what insurance investigator Amy Lynch must determine as she delves into the fallout from what at first appears to be an ordinary fire loss.

"It's a story that has a tragic beginning and a bittersweet ending. Leave it to Norton, who spent her entire career in the insurance industry, to make investigating claims seem exciting, a formidable task ... This fast-moving mystery injects thrills and sizzle into claims settlement."

—Kirkus Reviews

Avenging Madonna

An Amy Lynch Investigation

P.K. Norton

Visit our website at
www.StillwaterPress.com
for more information.

First Stillwater River Publications Edition

ISBN: 978-1-958217-42-9

1 2 3 4 5 6 7 8 9 10
Written by P.K. Norton
Published by Stillwater River Publications,
Pawtucket, RI, USA.

Names: Norton, P. K., author.
Title: Avenging Madonna / P.K. Norton
Description: First Stillwater River Publications edition. |
Pawtucket, RI, USA : Stillwater River Publications, [2022] |
Series: An Amy Lynch investigation
Identifiers: ISBN: 978-1-958217-42-9
Subjects: LCSH: Women insurance investigators--New England-
-Fiction. | Ranches--California--San Luis Obispo--Fiction. |
Cattle stealing--California--San Luis Obispo--Fiction. | Murder--
California--San Luis Obispo--Fiction. | LCGFT: Cozy mysteries.
| Detective and mystery fiction.
Classification: LCC: PS3614.O78266 A94 2022 | DDC: 813/.6-
-dc23

For Tom, whose devious yet logical mind helped me immeasurably as I plotted and planned.

*With special thanks to: **Jane** and **Lindsy** for their usual help and support; **Sue** for spending time with me researching and enjoying the Madonna Inn; **Clint Pearce**, Real Estate Manager at Madonna Enterprises for sharing with me his knowledge of the inn and the art of cattle raising as well as for putting up my incessant questions; and, as always, to **Jack** for inspiring me to set out on this adventure.*

The Madonna Inn, a delightful resort and spa in San Luis Obispo CA is very real. Both the Inn and the town have a rich and fascinating history that has been the inspiration for this story. The story itself is fiction.

Chapter 1

Sounds did strange things in the hills at night, particularly when there was a wind. They blew around a person as if from all directions at once, making it nearly impossible to determine their source. Or their meaning. Such was the case tonight. The air carried with it the howls of coyotes, grey wolves and the occasional cougar as well. Vultures, rarely observed in the sky at night, responded from above, interrupted off and on by an errant hoot owl.

These sounds could spook even the gentlest of horses. Gus stroked his mount's mane and spoke softly to reassure her the noises posed no threat.

Amid this disharmony, Gus's ears struggled to zero in on one particular sound, the cry of an animal in distress. This was different from the other noises. It was somehow sadder. And at the same time, more desperate. But where was this lament coming from? And why? Gus detected fear in the cry as well. But fear from what?

Gus hated working at night. Granted it was only every third night; it could have been worse. Still, he missed the camaraderie of the daytime shift, the companionship of his fellow ranch hands. He was, after all, a social being.

There was a second cowhand assigned to the shift with him. They were supposed to work together, having each other's back, but

Brody didn't buy into the buddy system plan. He preferred to separate from Gus and wander off by himself, insisting that was better because they could cover more ground that way. It wasn't how they were supposed to work; Brody did it anyway. Gus was fed up. He had spoken to Brody about it more than once, but to no avail. The next time it happened, Gus planned to complain to the foreman.

Tonight was the final affront. Brody he had failed to show up at all.

Gus was on his own. And that wasn't good. The loneliness was bad enough. The potential perils lurking in the hills made it all the worse. The darkness created a gloom which was almost palpable, particularly on a cloudy night like this. It came at him like a threat, a warning of impending danger.

He shivered, more from unease than from the cold. He strained his ears to locate the source of his concern – a low, mournful cry, a plea for help coming from a young steer which had lost its way in the hills. Gus needed to locate the animal and do whatever it took to bring it to safety. Not an easy task for one person alone in the dark. He dismounted and tethered his horse to a tree then continued on foot.

The lantern he normally carried with him had gone missing from the barn. All he had tonight was his flashlight. And that was dying on him fast, the batteries apparently on their way out. This should not be happening. Gus had changed the batteries only yesterday. He was sure of it. Nevertheless, the light was definitely forsaking him now, just when he needed it most.

Gus gritted his teeth and forged on in the ever-failing light. He had no choice. It was critical to rescue the animal before it succumbed to whatever mishap had befallen it. The ranch had lost too many steers over the recent months, sometimes as many as one a week. They couldn't sustain this trend for long. The cattle business was difficult enough these days without having to deal with missing or injured stock. Gus needed to find this latest victim – fast.

AVENGING MADONNA

Steeling himself against the wind and the chill, he aimed his dimming flashlight in what he believed to be the right direction. A sudden depression in the ground nearly caused him to trip.

He cursed the uneven terrain. He cursed the wind, and the dark and the cold. He cursed his flashlight for its impending and untimely death. He cursed his boss for putting him on night duty. His curses fell on deaf ears in the darkness.

A sudden movement somewhere nearby startled Gus. He aimed his flashlight at the ground ahead of him. A skunk darted across his path and disappeared in the darkness, leaving his scent behind.

The steer's cries became louder. Gus knew he must be getting close. He stepped forward uneasily, all too aware of the potential dangers in the surrounding landscape – ravines sneaking up when least expected, difficult to spot even in the daylight. The clouds overhead only made it harder. The cries became clearer, more intense. The animal had to be somewhere nearby.

The clouds began to dissipate and the moon appeared. It was nearly full, almost bright enough to compensate for his flashlight, now nearly dead in his hands. With the help of the moonlight, Gus spotted movement in the distance. The missing steer?

Gus concentrated on the sound of the animal's ever-weaker cries, straining to eliminate any other random noise. He concentrated so intently that he failed to hear the soft footsteps approaching him from behind. A particularly strong gust of wind assailed him. Or was it something more than just the wind? He took a tentative step forward, but his foot never touched ground. With a cry of surprise, Gus pitched headlong into a ravine. His body thudded onto the ground twenty feet below.

A new sound emerged in the night. A man in dark clothing standing at the top whistled to himself as he turned to set Gus' horse free and headed off into the dark.

Chapter 2

I awoke with a jolt to my head and a crick in my neck. Where the heck was I? Definitely not in my own bed. Opening my eyes brought it all back to me in a flash. My flight from Boston had just landed in San Francisco. And I had slept through pretty much all seven hours of it.

That was a good thing. I had barely slept the night before, then risen before dawn to catch a 6:00 AM flight. I checked my phone for the local time. Just before 10:00. I'd already been up for what seemed like ages. And I was ravenous. There had been no time for breakfast before leaving home. Then I slept through whatever passed for lunch on the plane. My stomach was not happy.

I couldn't think about that now. I needed to grab my luggage and locate the terminal for the plane to my ultimate destination – San Luis Obispo. I roused myself from my drowsiness and forged on.

As I neared the luggage carousel, a disembodied female voice called out on the public address system, "Passenger Amy Lynch, please contact the SLO Airlines ticket counter." *Oh dear! What in the world was that about?* I grabbed my phone to comply and was notified that my departure gate had been changed to number 6. No big deal. At least the flight hadn't been delayed. I retrieved my suitcase and set off in search of gate 6.

AVENGING MADONNA

An hour and a half later, I left the rental car counter at the San Luis Obispo Airport armed with the keys to a Mustang convertible as well as a local map. My stomach growled. I did my best to ignore it. Instead, I breathed in the fresh air and checked out my surroundings. The airport was small and friendly. It had a restaurant with a view of the runway. I liked that – so much friendlier than the hustle and bustle of most airports. I would have liked to pop in there for a bite. Maybe another time. Business first.

The drive to the Madonna Inn, where I would be staying, took less than fifteen minutes. That didn't give me much time to wake up fully from my lengthy nap and get my head on straight for the job that awaited me. Oh well, I could wing it for a while.

One of the best perks of my job was that, as manager of the claims department, I could pick and choose which insurance losses to investigate myself. This one was a no-brainer. It involved cattle rustling - something I had never dealt with before. I seldom passed up the opportunity to delve into a topic outside of the usual array of fires, thefts and storm damage.

I was curious to learn why the Madonna Inn owned cattle at all, never mind why they were being stolen, or rustled.

Not only that, but I had heard that the Madonna Inn was a delightfully quirky place. It would be fun to see for myself exactly what that meant. All I knew so far was that the men's room in the main building had a urinal designed as a waterfall. I wasn't sure why that was so, but was also unsure whether or not I wanted to know that answer. At any rate, it'd be fun to check it out. Maybe even take a selfie in front of it. That would be a big hit at the office.

One way or another, I expected to have an interesting week.

As I steered my rental car into the driveway to the Madonna Inn and took a good look around, my first thought was: *I'm not quite sure how I feel about these old-fashioned lamp posts painted Pepto Bismol pink.* My second thought was: *What are all those emergency vehicles doing here?* I was fully awake now. My ears were assaulted with the combined shrieks of police vehicles and an ambulance. My day became more interesting in the blink of an eye.

I pulled over on the narrow road to allow an ambulance on its way out of the inn to pass. A vehicle labelled Sheriff, San Luis Obispo County followed close behind. This was not a good sign. I hoped to hell it was nothing which would complicate my investigation. And I was pretty sure I was kidding myself that it wouldn't. Things seldom worked that way for me.

There was only one way to find out what was going on. I headed toward a sign that said: Office. It was an interesting looking building, constructed of both wood and stone. The ground floor was round, the second more octagonal. For some reason, it made me think of a multi-tiered birthday cake topped with white and pink frosting. Fanciful, in a fun kind of way.

The office itself proved to be more utilitarian than whimsical. Not to mention unattended at the moment. A bell jingled to announce my arrival. Nobody appeared to notice. I was alone in the room. There was a bowl of Halloween candy on the counter. And it was full of peanut butter cups. My favorite. I grabbed a handful, then quickly stuffed one into my mouth and the rest into my pocket.

Unhappy voices coming from an adjoining room assured me there were indeed people nearby. I tuned into their conversation.

"This is terrible," a male voice whined. "What are we going to do?"

"The only thing we can do," a woman answered him. "Stay calm and carry on. Business as usual. We cannot go upsetting our guests."

A twenty-something woman with dark eyes and lustrous black hair piled high on her head emerged from the back room. She was nearly as short as me, and full-bodied without appearing chunky. She wore a white peasant blouse and a colorful southwestern skirt. Nice look, except perhaps for the sneakers. I swallowed my peanut butter cup as quickly as I could.

"Hello," the woman said. She smiled in my direction, then turned to the man who followed behind her. "Gotta run, Steve. My break was over five minutes ago. See you later." She hurried to the door.

"Good afternoon," the man said to me. "Welcome to the Madonna Inn. So sorry to keep you waiting. What can I do for you?" He was forty-ish, tall and fair, with perfect teeth and an adorable smile. The badge on his navy-blue blazer identified him as Steve Damon.

"I'm Amy Lynch from New England Casualty and Indemnity," I said. "Here to investigate your cattle rustling claim. I just saw a sheriff's car and the ambulance rushing out of here. What happened?"

Steve frowned. "From what little I know at this point, there was an accident. One of our ranch hands was found at the bottom of a ravine this morning. Dead. A fellow named Gus Cameron. It's all a terrible shock. Gus was a super nice fellow. He always had a smile for everybody, as well as a good story or two. And boy did that guy love to talk. Everybody liked him. I can't believe he's dead."

How did he die?" I asked. *Was he caught rustling and shot?*

"From what I hear, he fell last night," Steve said. "Out in the hills. Into a really deep ravine. It seems he cracked his skull and bled to death."

I stopped him right there. "What in the world was he doing out in the hills at night?"

"Watching for rustlers. That's when they're most likely to strike."

"Alone?" I asked. *If that's their idea of security here, no wonder there was a rustling problem.*

"I'm afraid so. There normally would be at least two guys working the night watch in those hills. It seems that Brody, the other guy on the night shift, called in sick yesterday. At least that's what he says."

"And they didn't send somebody out there to take his place?" I asked, grateful that my new friend Steve also liked to talk. I definitely liked to listen to anything and everything when I was on a case, whether it appeared to be relevant or not. Being nosy is a big part of my job. Perhaps my favorite part.

"Brody claims his call went straight to voicemail and he left a message for Jess. The trouble is that Jess never heard the message. Either it got deleted in error or Brody is lying to save his own ass. Oops, sorry. Pardon the language. Either way, nobody knew Gus was alone out there. It gets pretty dark in the hills at night. Particularly when it's cloudy, like it was last night. Without light from the moon and the stars, it simply isn't safe out there. You never know what can happen. Until it does. And by then it's too late. Like now."

"I'm so sorry to hear that. This must be very difficult for all of you," I said, hoping to prompt him into telling me more.

Steve nodded. "That's for darn sure. But, like I was just saying to Rosa, life goes on. We've all got to keep on keeping on. We still have an inn to run, guests to greet. That has to be our priority. It wouldn't do for our guests to get upset."

I could have sworn I'd just heard Rosa saying that very thing to him. Silly me.

"Speaking of guests," I said, "I need to check in. Then I have a 1:30 meeting with Clint Jennings."

Steve nodded. "Right. I'm afraid this isn't the best way to welcome you. Things have been pretty hectic all morning."

"I'm sure they have."

"I'm sorry to tell you," Steve continued, "that I have two pieces of not-so-good news for you. Now, don't get me wrong, please. It's nothing terrible. Just a little inconvenient, if you know what I mean."

I didn't know what he meant, but was pretty sure he was about to tell me. "What is it?"

He frowned. "First of all, your room isn't quite ready. It should have been done by now, but with all the commotion this morning, things sort of fell behind. We've got you in the Yahoo room. You're going to love it there."

The Yahoo room? Yikes! I'd heard that this inn was quirky and fun, with each room having a different, and interesting, theme. But Yahoo? Really? I was a bit worried about what the theme might be. "The Yahoo room," I repeated. "Sounds interesting." *And perhaps a bit risqué depending upon why anyone would be shouting Yahoo.*

The look on my face must have clued Steve in to my thoughts. "Yeah. Right. It's room number 132, at the top of the hill. The décor is straight out of the days of cowboys and cattle drives. It's like what you'd find at the end of the trail, after a long day riding the range. You can cool off in the rock waterfall shower before falling asleep on the authentic 'Buckboard bed.'"

It sounded to me like Steve had done a wonderful job of memorizing the Inn's brochure. I smiled and gave him silent credit for his initiative.

"The room is filled with memorabilia from those days," he continued. "You'll love it. I expect you can get into it within an hour or so. I am so sorry about the wait. We usually manage to do better than that."

After that description, I was sorry as well. Couldn't wait to see the buckboard bed. "Not a problem," I told him. I could be gracious when necessary. "I can spend some time exploring the grounds here. It looks like an interesting place." I also wanted to get something to eat. Soon. A couple of peanut butter cups just didn't do the trick.

Steve handed me the room key and a map of the property. He pointed to a few locations. "Here's your room. There's parking right outside your door. I'll text you when the room is ready for you. In the meantime, please stick to this immediate area for now - the shops, restaurants, spa, gardens and whatnot." He pointed these places out on the map. "You better stay away from the hills at least until the cops are done out there."

"Of course," I said. "But you said two pieces of news. What else do I need to know?"

"Right. I almost forgot. Clint is going to be tied up for a while, dealing with the authorities. He needs to reschedule your meeting with him until later, like around 4:00 or so. It can't be helped. I hope that's all right with you. He asked if you could meet him then, in the cocktail lounge. It's called the Silver Bar. You can see it on this map here." He pointed to the lounge in question.

Interesting spot for a business meeting, I thought. But what the heck?

"And then Clint is hoping you can join him for dinner," Steve added.

I smiled. "Sounds good." *And in the meantime, I'll get the lay of the land and do a bit of snooping. You never know what you might find. And how it might relate to my case.*

Chapter 3

I checked out the map Steve had given me, then drove up the hill. My room was located near the top, overlooking the pool and spa area. Also overlooking a vast expanse of property with some lovely hills in the background. No cattle in sight at the moment, but I was pretty sure they had to be out there somewhere, or I wouldn't be here checking into their disappearance.

I took a moment to enjoy the view, then parked the Mustang and headed back down the road on foot. Fresh air and exercise would do me a lot of good after sitting in an airplane for so many hours. It would also be a good way to familiarize myself with the premises. You never knew what might prove to be important. Perhaps I'd find something untoward along the way. One can always hope.

The property was large and quite lovely, filled with well-manicured shrubs and big beautiful red azaleas. They had a pleasant, spicy scent. Nice.

I chose the route that the map indicated would take me past a variety of attractions - basketball and tennis courts, a pond, a secret garden and something listed as the Lion's Den. That piqued my interest. The pond was picturesque, peaceful and relaxing. The tennis courts were painted Pepto Bismol pink. Why not? They fit right in with the street lights. I actually liked the effect. Fun colors do tend to brighten up a person's day.

The garden wasn't much of a secret, but you could play corn hole there, or croquet or bocce ball. A nice touch, particularly if you have kids with you. What was billed as the lion's den appeared to be nothing more than a shed. That was a disappointment. Maybe there was an interesting story behind it. I would look further into that when I got the chance.

Arriving back at the building which held the office, I re-checked my map. The location also housed a bakery, two restaurants and at least two gift shops. Not needing any gifts at the moment, I opted for food.

It was a little past noon, or 3:00 according to my growling stomach. Time differences could do that to a person.

The Copper Café was easy to find. And difficult to miss. The shiny pink seats at both the counter and the tables took care of that. There was no question as to what was the signature color of the Madonna Inn. Pink was ubiquitous, and a bit startling at first, but it definitely made the place look whimsical, not to mention intriguing. I couldn't help but wonder who could have chosen these colors. Or why?

The café was oddly quiet for lunch time. It had a faint, and not unpleasant, aroma of fried food. That made me all the more hungry. An older couple in tee shirts and shorts sat in one corner of the room. A younger couple with two small, and surprisingly well-behaved, children occupied another. I chose a table for two and sat with my back to the wall. All the better to observe my surroundings. I didn't want to miss a thing.

A twenty-something girl with short blond curls approached my table. She was dressed the same as the woman I had seen in the office – white peasant blouse and colorful southwestern skirt. Must be the official uniform. Her eyes were red and her skin blotchy, as if she had been crying. "Hello," she said as she handed me a menu. "How are you today?"

AVENGING MADONNA

Before I could answer the girl, she let out a large, noisy sob and ran toward the door to the kitchen. The dark-haired woman I had seen in the office reached out and hugged her. "There, there, Honey," she said. "I know how you feel. It's awful. And very, very sad. But you need to pull yourself together for now. We can't go upsetting our guests, or pretty soon we won't have any. And we all need these jobs, don't we?"

"I know," the girl replied. "I'm trying hard. Really I am. But it's just so hard. What am I going to do?"

"You're going to do what we all have to do. Stay strong and carry on."

The waitress sobbed and nodded. "I know. You're right. I'll try harder. Promise."

"Now go into the kitchen and dry your eyes," The woman told her. "I'll cover your tables for a little while."

The waitress disappeared into the kitchen. The other woman approached my table. Her employee badge identified her as Rosa Vazquez. "I'm sorry about that. We're having a difficult day here. One of our co-workers died last night. From what I heard, it was some sort of freak accident. He and Luisa were good friends."

"I heard there had been an accident. I'm so very sorry," I told her.

Rosa looked me in the eye. "Didn't I see you in the office a while ago?"

"That's right. I was checking in. I'm Any Lynch. I'm from the inn's insurance company, here to investigate the cattle rustling claim. It seems I arrived at a bad time."

"Well, Amy Lynch, it's nice to meet you."

"Likewise, Rosa," I said. "Is there any chance you might have a few minutes to chat with me? I'd be interested in anything you could tell me about the rustling problem, or the inn in general, or that poor fellow who passed away." *It never hurt to ask about anything. Or everything.*

"Why don't you order first?" Rosa said. "Then we can have a nice chat while your lunch is being prepared. Can I get you some coffee?"

"No thanks." I scanned the menu hungrily. "How about a double bacon cheeseburger, onion rings and sweet potato fries? I'm famished."

"Anything to drink?"

"A diet cola. I need to watch my weight."

Rosa smiled at my feeble attempt at levity. "Coming right up." She ordered my food then returned to my table with a cola and took a seat. "So, Amy Lynch, what can I tell you?"

"Anything you know about what has been happening around here."

She furrowed her brow. "I'm afraid I don't know anything at all concerning the cattle disappearing. Working here in the restaurant, we don't deal much with the ranch business. Or know much about what's going on out in the hills. Only what we hear from the cowboys."

That was understandable yet disappointing. I decided I might as well learn anything I could about the goings-on in general, just in case everything was somehow connected. "What about the fellow who died last night?" I asked. "Have you heard much about what happened?"

Rosa shook her head. "Nobody knows much of anything for sure. From what I heard, the ranch hands on the morning shift came across Gus's horse when they were heading out earlier today. The horse was saddled up, but had no rider. They set out to look for Gus. Followed the cries of the vultures. Found Gus at the bottom of a deep ravine way out in the hills. It looks like he fell and hit his head." She frowned. "He never should have been out there alone in the dark. I don't know what's wrong with management here to let something like that happen. There should always be at least two hands in those hills at night. No matter what."

That sounded like a no-brainer to me. "Do you know why there wasn't somebody with him?"

She frowned. "What I heard on the rumor mill was that Brody, the guy who was supposed to work that shift with Gus, never showed up last night. And nobody got sent out to cover for him."

"Oh dear. Do you have any idea how that happened?"

Rosa shrugged. "Somebody screwed up big time. That's for sure. And nobody's admitting to anything. The foreman at the ranch swears he never got a call that Brody wasn't coming in. My guess is that he was probably drunk – again. Jess, that is, not Brody. By the way, please don't quote me on that. I need this job."

"Is Jess the foreman?"

"Right. Jess Parker."

"What can you tell me about him?"

"Not much, I'm afraid. Except that he drinks a bit. I don't know him very well. From what I hear, though, he's mean and lazy. Not well liked. If you talk to him, please keep my name out of it."

That would be a 'when,' not an 'if.' "Will do. Did you know Gus well?" I asked.

"As well as I know any of the cowboys. Your waitress, Luisa, knew him a lot better. They've been an item for a while now. The poor girl is taking it really hard."

I pulled a pen and paper out of my purse to make a few notes. "What can you tell me about Gus? Was he a nice guy? Had he been working here long?"

Rosa closed her eyes in thought. "He'd been here the best part of two years. That's a long time for a ranch hand, at least the young ones. They tend to get restless and move around a lot. From what Luisa told me, Gus seemed to be happy enough here. Of course, that probably had something to do with his relationship with her, if you know what I mean."

I knew what she meant. "How did Gus get along with the other employees?"

"Everybody loved the guy - ranch hands, inn workers, even management. Gus had an easy way about him. He was friendly without being in your face. Always up for a laugh or a good time.

Always had a joke to tell, or a story. Yeah, he was popular. The poor guy hated it when he got stuck on the night shift, particularly since the other guy usually assigned with him isn't really the friendly sort. Brody's real quiet. Tends to keep to himself. Gus preferred his buddies from the daytime shifts. They're a rowdy bunch at times, but they're good people. And a lot of fun."

"Sounds like Gus will be missed," I said, hoping to keep Rosa talking.

"That's for sure. Between Gus's death and the cattle disappearing, things are looking a bit grim around here at the moment."

I was about to pursue the cattle topic when Rosa's phone dinged. "Oops," she said. "I've got a text." She scanned her message. "Your lunch is ready. I'll be right back."

As she dashed away to the kitchen, two groups of people showed up at the door. My guess was that, while Rosa might be right back, she wouldn't have any more time to chat. Pity. I made a few notes on what she had told me so far. I hoped I'd find another source of local gossip. And soon.

Chapter 4

I dug into my veritable feast of hot grease, loving every minute of it. I was so beyond hungry that I didn't even care about calories. Thank goodness for high metabolism. While I stuffed my face shamelessly, I texted Pete, the long-time and very special man in my life, to let him know I had arrived safely. I didn't fill him in on the goings-on at the Inn. Not in a text. That would involve far too much effort. My thumbs weren't all that agile. I preferred to email from my laptop. It let me use all ten fingers.

I knew I could also call Pete and speak with him directly, but I wasn't quite ready to do that yet. Not after our conversation last night. And my reaction to it. I munched on my sweet potato fries and revisited the conversation in my mind...

I was really looking forward to this trip. An intriguing claim to investigate – cattle rustling at an old inn in California. Nothing humdrum about that. It was also a visit to an area of California I didn't know, but which sounded interesting. This was supposed to be enhanced by having Pete at my side. It sounded like the perfect get-away. Exactly what I needed. Or so I thought at the time.

The claim was still out there awaiting investigation. I was eager to sink my teeth into it. A pleasant trip with Pete? That was not happening. And the sad truth was that I was fine with that. Actually, I was relieved. And therein lay the problem.

"I'm sorry, Ames," he had told me. "I can't go with you like we planned."

"Why not?" I asked.

"Because I need to meet with a client tomorrow."

"Isn't it something that could wait for a couple of days?" I asked, then immediately wondered why I'd bothered. And that bothered me.

"I'm afraid it can't wait." Pete hesitated for a moment, as if to gather his thoughts. "This issue came up rather suddenly for the client when he was arrested today. He's out on bail at the moment. Has a 2:00 date in court tomorrow. I have to speak with him before that, then accompany him to court. I need to be there for him. It's my job."

That made sense. "Of course you do, Pete. I get that," I said. "You're the new attorney in town. You've got a client with a problem that can't wait. I understand. You and I will plan another get-away sometime soon."

"I'm really sorry, Ames," he continued. "But you are right, as the new guy in town, my reputation is at stake. How I treat my first new client since taking over the practice could make or break me. I've got to get it right if I expect to succeed in a small town. There are other attorneys in the area. I need to be better than all of them. All the time."

When I didn't respond immediately, he added, "I can't tell you how disappointed I am. I was really looking forward to this trip, to some time alone with you exploring someplace new. Maybe my case will be settled quickly and I can join you in a day or two."

I gave that some thought. And wasn't sure how I felt about it.

Pete and I had been together for nearly five years now. He was my one and only serious romance since my fiancé Danny died in an auto accident in Key West. That seemed like forever ago now. Pete and I had a good thing going, at least until the past few months.

AVENGING MADONNA

Things began to change when he moved out of Boston, way out, into a place so small they called it a junction instead of a town. Pete had immediately taken to small town living. I had not. While I wasn't actually living with him, I did visit a lot.

I much preferred the energy, the urban vibe, of Cambridge, where I had lived for the past several years. Sadly, I hadn't admitted any of this to myself before. Perhaps I hadn't even realized it, until that moment. Then I knew I really wanted to go by myself, to have some time alone to rethink where my life was going – and perhaps have an adventure or two while I was away. Maybe even have a fling. Perhaps that would be good for me. *Oh, my! Where did that thought even come from?*

"Is there any chance you could put your trip off for a day or two?" Pete asked.

"I'm afraid not. The Madonna Inn is a good, long-term client. They've had a serious loss. They're expecting me tomorrow. And if I put that off for personal reasons, George would raise holy hell with the boss. He'd probably claim he should have been sent in my place. I can't deal with that."

"Is he giving you a hard time again?" Pete asked.

"It's more like still. He hates it when I take a plum assignment rather than delegating it to him."

"Which you did," Pete said. "Was that for business reasons, or just to piss him off?"

Partly to piss him off," I admitted. "But I also don't think he's got what it takes to deal with an important client. After all, I got promoted over him for a reason. And he has been a particularly royal pain in the butt lately. A lot worse than usual. As a matter of fact, I didn't even leave him in charge while I'll be away."

"Isn't it time for the two of you to put an end to that feud? I thought you had called a truce not so long ago, come to some sort of an arrangement that worked for both of you."

"So did I. It didn't last long."

"I'm sorry to hear that," he said.

"Me too. But even if I could send someone else, I wouldn't want to."

"How come?"

"Because I really want to go. I've never been to this part of California. I hear it's nice. And it's an interesting case. I'm looking forward to it."

"Well, since I can't go with you, I can at least take care of Sam while you're gone. After all, my back yard is like canine heaven to him."

I shook my head, then realized that Pete couldn't see that action over the phone. "Sorry. No can do. Peggy already offered. You know how much she loves to dog-sit for me. Besides, Sam is already at her house." Technically, Peggy was my assistant. In truth, she was so much more than that to me – good friend, dog-sitter, pretty much whatever I needed at any given time – at the office or anywhere else. And Sam, my scruffy mutt and best friend, just loved spending time with her.

Pete was silent for what seemed like forever. He tended to do that when he had some weighty problem on his mind. Finally, he said, "Well, I guess that's that then. I'll see you when you return. And miss you in the meantime."

"I'll miss you too," I said. It wasn't until after we'd hung up that I admitted to myself that may not be exactly true. But I'd be damned if I'd admit it out loud. Instead, I lay awake most of the night alternately scolding myself for feeling the way I did and applauding myself for admitting it, particularly the part about having a fling.

So there I sat in the Copper Café, swallowing the last of my lunch, thinking about the next few days. Looking forward to them, actually. I had an interesting claim to investigate, a chance to learn about both inn-keeping and cattle rustling, and some time alone to work on getting my priorities straight. My phone dinged. A text from Steve Damon at the front desk saying that my room was ready. Perfect timing.

I paid my bill and set out back up the hill to check out the Yahoo room.

Chapter 5

I walked to my room by way of the mysterious Lion's Den, aka "the shed." This time I got lucky, perhaps in more ways than one. As I approached the shed, I heard voices coming from somewhere nearby. I turned to see a rear view of two men I guessed were cowboys, one tall, one short. Both were dressed in jeans, leather vests and cowboy boots. I rather liked the look. They were putting a fresh coat of paint on the Lion's Den. The taller of the two turned as I approached. He was sporting a large silver belt buckle with turquoise stones in it. Nice. He also had truly great buns.

"Good afternoon, Ma'am," he said. "Lovely day, don't you think?" He had pale brown hair just a bit too long. It gave him a devil-may-care look. He also had a gorgeous smile and sparkly green eyes almost as nice as Pete's. Perhaps even nicer. I guessed him to be in his late thirties.

I smiled back. "Yes. It certainly is nice."

The shorter fellow had thick white hair and a weathered face. He nodded in my direction, grunted and resumed painting.

The hunk preferred to chat with me. "I don't remember seeing you around here before, Ma'am. You just arrive?"

I ignored the Ma'am. "Yes. I checked in this morning."

"Well then, welcome to the Madonna Inn. I'm Lance. It's nice to meet you." He reached out to shake my hand.

Lance? Somehow the name seemed out of place on a cattle ranch. Nevertheless, it suited this guy. "Nice to meet you, Lance. And please call me Amy. I usually prefer that to Ma'am."

"Gotcha." There was that lovely smile again. "So, what brings you to the Madonna Inn, Amy?"

"Business." I handed him my card. "I'm looking into the cattle rustling claim."

"Right. Clint said a representative from the insurance company was coming. He didn't mention that it'd be someone as lovely as you."

Oh my! Flattery will get you everywhere, Lance. But don't lay it on too thick. "Some time within the next day or two, I will need to ask you a few questions. I really don't know very much about cattle ranching – or rustling."

"That would be my pleasure. Just let me know where and when and what you need to know. I'll be there with bells on."

That might be something I'd like to see. "Will do." I said. *And with pleasure.* I took a look at the shed. "Actually, there is one question I hope you can answer for me now."

"Sure thing. I'll do my best. What do you want to know?"

"Why is this shed called the Lion's Den?"

Lance let out a loud guffaw. "I get that question a lot. Years ago, when Mr. Madonna first bought this property, he had a pet lion. This is where he kept it. People tell me the place didn't look so much like a shed in those days. I guess we'll have to take their word for that."

"Thanks, Lance. That's good to know. Not to mention rather cool."

He smiled. "Just one more thing that makes the Madonna Inn unique."

No argument there. I checked the time on my phone. "I better head to my room now. I need to get to work."

"See you soon." He turned to resume his work with the older fellow. I continued making my way up the hill.

The Yahoo room was a sight to behold, particularly the bed. It had a high headboard with a large set of cattle horns at the top of it. The footboard was the front of an old buckboard wagon – with two wheels, a seat for two and an old lantern. The carpet was bright red, as were the drapes behind the bed, though they had flecks of gold in them as well. The shower looked like a rock waterfall. Unique, to say the least. It'd make a good story when I got home. I took a picture with my phone.

My next move should have been to call Pete. I dialed Peggy instead, lying to myself that the job at hand had to come first. I got her voice mail. Then I remembered the time difference. My phone said 3:30. That meant it was 6:30 in New England. I dialed Peggy again, but this time at her home.

"Howdy, Pardner," she said. "How's life on the ranch?"

I laughed. "I believe it's going to be quite an interesting adventure here. I'm eager to sink my teeth into my investigation. Also, this place is a hoot. And delightfully so."

"Please explain."

"A large part of the inn is painted bright pink," I began, then went on to provide her with a detailed description of the grounds I had seen so far. Then I described my room.

"That actually could be kind of fun," Peggy said.

"It is. And the views are gorgeous. My room is near the top of a hill. It overlooks both the inn and some pretty spectacular hills in the background. There is also a lovely waterfall."

"Sounds nice so far," she said.

"It would be," I said, "except that I arrived in the middle of a tragedy." I told her what little I knew about the ranch hand's death and the chaos that accompanied it.

"Good grief, Amy. Let's hope that doesn't interfere with your investigation. Remember, your job is to deal with the cattle rustling claim. You need to concentrate on that."

Sometimes Peggy sounded more like my mother than my assistant.

"Yes, Ma'am. Will do. Although there's a better than even chance that the two things may be connected. The timing is rather curious. My gut tells me they're somehow linked. After all, as you know, there is no such thing as coincidence."

"So you keep telling me," she said. "Nevertheless, you better begin by dealing with the rustling. If that fellow's death is somehow involved, you'll figure it out quickly enough."

"Actually, I am planning on spending some time getting my head around what information we currently have on the claim and putting together my questions for the general manager. It should be interesting to learn what he has to say. I'm meeting with him in half an hour," I told her.

Peggy let out a gasp. "Does that mean you're going to sit down at your laptop and study the files on line?"

"It does." The technophobe within me cringed slightly at the thought, but I was determined to make it work.

"And you're going to record the conversation on your phone like I showed you instead of taking written notes?"

"Sure. Just hit the Voice Memo button, right?"

"Well wonders never cease," she said. "And welcome to the new millennium."

I laughed.

"That reminds me," Peggy continued, "I've been doing a bit of research on cattle ranching in general, hoping I'll learn something which will help you to put an accurate value on this loss."

"And when have you found the time to do that?" I asked. "Are things that quiet at the office?"

"Not really, but I thought it might be helpful. I made the time."

"You are good. So what did you learn?"

Peggy let out a large breath, then said, "As of yesterday, the average price for a steer was approximately $1,000. But that's not all you need to look at. There are residual values involved as well."

Hmmm. "Such as?" I asked.

"By-products."

"Oh?"

"Oh, indeed. The deal is that when a steer is processed at the ranch rather than sold, there is obviously the value of the meat. The surprise is that there are also a number of by-products. And these can have considerable value as well."

"By-products, huh? Such as?" I asked, intrigued by the thought.

"It's mostly hides and tallow. And that's all I can tell you at the moment. I had plans last evening, so my research ended there. At least for now."

I considered this new information. "Thanks. Please keep it up. This could make a huge difference in how this claim plays out. You are good."

"I try," she said. I could hear her smiling at the praise.

"On another subject, how's Sam?" I asked.

"He's the happiest mutt in town. I do love dog-sitting for you. Sam and I are having a wonderful time together."

"Give him a big hug for me."

"Will do," Peggy said, then asked, "Have you spoken with Pete?"

I sighed. "Not yet. He's next on my list."

"Good. He called me first thing this morning, supposedly to arrange to visit with Sam. He misses you already. Pete, that is. Although I'm pretty sure that Sam does as well. Anyway, Pete is feeling terrible about not being able to join you in California. I hate the fact that he's so lonely so soon."

I knew what she meant. "Poor guy. I'll make it a point to keep in touch with him regularly. But I am beginning to think that maybe I can do a better job with this claim if I don't have him as a distraction."

"Oh?" Peggy said. "OK, let's have it, Amy. Tell me what's really going on."

She knew me far too well. I gave her an abbreviated account of my current feelings about Pete. For some reason, I also told her about my meeting with Lance.

"Lance?" she laughed. "You've got to love that name on a cowboy. Sure sounds like he got your attention big time."

"And then some," I admitted. "I couldn't help myself. He is charming and adorable, and hopefully, available."

"Amy Lynch! Are you considering having a fling?" The gasp in her voice was audible.

The best answer I could give her was, "You never know."

"That's somewhat of a surprise," Peggy said. "Although I do think it might just be good for you."

For better or for worse, I thought so as well. "I better go now," I told her. "It's time to get ready for my meeting."

I hung up, then dialed Pete. Voicemail. That was a relief. I left a boring message, promised to call again later, then began prepping for my meeting with Clint.

Chapter 6

Clint Jennings stood as I entered the Silver Bar at 4:00. He was the general manager of operations at Madonna Enterprises, which included both the inn and the cattle business. He was well over six feet and lean, in a muscle-bound sort of way. His dark brown hair was laced with gray around the edges; his face told me he'd spent a lot of time in the sun. The best thing about him at first glance was that his eyes appeared to smile along with his mouth.

I particularly liked the fact that his rugged good looks were in sharp contrast to the less-than-subtle pink décor of the bar.

"Ms. Lynch, I presume?"

I shook his proffered hand. "Hello. It's nice to meet you."

We sat at a small cocktail table with pale pink armchairs.

"What are you drinking?" Clint asked.

I took a quick look at the cocktail menu. My favorite whiskey was listed. "I'll have a shot of Black Barrel, with water on the side." *Why not? I wasn't driving.*

He laughed. "I like a woman who knows good hooch. I believe I'll join you." He signaled the bartender and placed our order. When our drinks arrived, he lifted his glass. "So, Ms. Lynch, welcome to the Madonna Inn and cattle ranch. I'm afraid we didn't give you much of a welcome earlier. We'll have to see what we can do to improve on that."

I sipped my drink, then said. "Not a problem. You obviously had other priorities this morning."

A dark cloud passed briefly across Clint's face. "That's for darn sure. Anyway, we're glad you're here. I know it's to do a job, but I hope you'll find some time enjoy your stay here as well. So, how about we get our business out of the way first, then we can have a nice friendly chat over dinner?"

"I'm looking forward to that," I said as I referred to my notes. "Let's start at the beginning. How many head of cattle do you normally have at the ranch?"

"About 150 head," he replied. "Give or take a few."

I made a quick note. "And how many cows is that? Or do you call them steers?"

"We call them both," he said. "It depends. Cows are females, steers are castrated males. There are also bulls. They're not castrated."

"And you use the word 'head' to describe them all?" I asked.

"Right. It's easier that way. Takes only one word, not three."

That made sense. "I see."

I thought this over, then said, "So what you're telling me is that a single animal, be it cow or bull or steer, is considered one head of cattle."

His grin broadened. "You've got it," he said.

"But why that particular word?" I asked.

Clint shrugged. "Beats me. That's just the way it has always been."

That struck me as odd, but I could deal with it. Time to move on. "And when did you first realize some of your cattle had gone missing?"

Clint hesitated a moment, then said, "Nearly three months ago, I'd say."

Three months? Really? "Why did you wait so long to file a claim?"

He lowered his eyes. "We didn't realize what was going on at first. It took us a few months to figure it out."

That made me question their operating procedures. "Don't you people count your stock on a regular basis?" I realized a second too late how rude that sounded. Luckily, Clint didn't seem to mind.

"We do," he said. "The thing is, around here the regular basis has always been once a month or so. No rigid schedule. That has worked well enough for us until recently. There is always some slight discrepancy, you see. It's easy to miss a cow or two when we're herding them up. Some little calf may be hiding in the bushes somewhere. Or one or two head could be wandering about pretty much anywhere. It happens all the time. We've got over 1,000 acres here. They all show up eventually, or at least they did until now."

"Do you mean they are able to get past your fences?" I asked.

He shook his head. "No fences to get past."

That didn't set very well with me. "But why not? Wouldn't simple wire fences eliminate the problem for you?"

"Maybe. But solving that problem would bring on a few new ones."

"Like what?"

Clint sipped his drink, then replied, "Barbed wire can injure an animal. We can't afford to take that risk. If it doesn't kill them outright, it sure can reduce their value come sale time. Also, wire is easy to cut and expensive to replace. Just doesn't work for us. And it's never been a problem before. Not until recently anyway."

"So what happened to make it become a problem?" I asked. "Did something change?"

Clint stared at his hands. "Damned if I know. But all of a sudden, the numbers were just too far off."

"How far is too far off?"

He scratched his chin. "Like I was telling you, nobody worries if we're off by a couple of head. Maybe even five or six. That's pretty normal. It all resolves itself eventually. But anything more than five or six head would sound an alarm. And it did."

I'd take his word for that, at least for now. "When was the last time you counted your stock?"

"Two weeks ago. Just before we filed our claim."

"And how many head were there at that time?" I asked.

"Only 118." He frowned as he said this. "Never had that big a discrepancy before. That's why we contacted you folks."

I checked my notes. "Are you telling me that 32 cows had been rustled?"

Clint shook his head. "Not exactly."

Now I was confused. "What do you mean?"

"We're down by 32 head. That's a fact. But it's not all from rustling. There's also the dead ones."

I dropped my pen. "Did you say dead?"

"I'm afraid so," Clint said with a solemn nod. "That's the latest development. Just started a week ago. And it makes no damn sense."

I was almost afraid to ask, "How did they die?"

"Slit throats."

Holy shit! "Slit throats?" I echoed.

"I'm afraid so."

That added a whole new dimension to my claim investigation. A rather upsetting one.

"Do you think it could be a mountain lion or some other predator?"

Clint shook his head. "Nope. Can't be. The cuts are too clean, damn near surgical. And once that's done, whoever it is that's killing our animals just leaves them in the hills to die."

"But that makes no sense at all. Why would rustlers do that? How could they possibly make a profit?"

"They couldn't," Clint said. "Rustlers want the whole animal alive. For the money. This has got to be somebody else. Somebody with something else in mind. Damned if I know what, though. But when you think about it, at least this way, the ranch gets some money out of it."

"What do you mean?"

"Meat isn't the only product you get from cattle, you know. There's also the by-products."

"You mean like hides and tallow?" I asked.

It was fun to see the surprised look on his face. "Well, well, I see the lady has done her homework."

I smiled and let him believe that was the case, silently blessing Peggy for her diligence. "I know a little bit about these by-products," I said, feigning modesty. "I'd love to hear the details if you don't mind."

Apparently that worked just fine for Clint. "Well, these by-products have always been a big part of the cattle business, all the way back to when folks used tallow candles. And in the old days, hides were actually a medium of exchange in these parts."

I nodded my understanding and made a note to discuss this in detail with Peggy. It would surely figure into the value of this claim.

"Aside from by-products, how much is an individual animal worth?" I asked Clint, wondering if he would confirm what Peggy had said.

"They normally go for about $1,000 each."

Bingo! It was good to know Clint wasn't inflating values to increase the claim payout.

I referred to my notes and did some quick math. "So if you have lost 32 head, some stolen, some killed, we're talking about a loss of around $32,000, give or take a little for the value of the tallow or the hide of the animals left here to die."

"The give or take could be more than just a little," he said. "But that sums it up pretty well."

"And out of the 32 animals you've lost, how many were killed and left here?"

"There were 26 actually stolen. The other 6 were left to die."

I'd work that math out with Peggy.

"Just a few more questions," I said.

"Shoot." He gestured with his hand mimicking firing a pistol.

"Have you reported all this to the authorities?"

"Yes, Ma'am. Of course we did. Right away."

No surprise there, but I needed to confirm it for the record. "Have you taken measures to prevent further problems?"

Clint nodded. "Sure have."

"Specifically, what have you done?"

"Added the night shift."

"Has that helped?" I asked.

"Maybe," he said. "Too soon to tell for sure."

Time to broach a different subject. "Do you have any thoughts on who may be responsible for the rustling? And the killing?"

Clint's eyebrows shot up. "What do you mean?"

"I mean – do you have any enemies? Maybe a competitor who would like to see you go out of business?"

"Can't think of anybody off-hand. Let me give that some thought."

"One final question," I said. "And it's a tough one."

"What?"

I took a deep breath, then said, "Do you think it could be an inside job?"

That brought a serious frown to Clint's face. "Anything's possible, I guess. Sure hope not, though. That'd be the ultimate betrayal." He let out a sigh. "Anyway, how about we adjourn to the dining room and continue our conversation while we eat some dinner? I don't know about you, but I'm starving. And I can guarantee you one hell of a tasty steak."

Food sounded good to me. Besides, I couldn't wait to see what the dining room looked like. If what I had seen so far of the inn was any indication, I guessed it might be a sight to behold. Swallowing the last of my whiskey, I stood and followed Clint into the restaurant.

Chapter 7

The Gold Rush Steak House did not disappoint. It was as bold and bright and fanciful as everything I had seen at the Madonna Inn so far. The entire room was sparkly and pink. The color was no surprise by now; the sparkles were rather delightful. There were angels in the chandeliers, surrounded by tiny white lights. The tables were small and round and cozy-looking, all encircled by cushy couches, pink of course. The restaurant was quiet this early in the evening. Soft music was playing in the background. All in all, it was pretty nice.

As soon as we settled in, a sommelier showed up at our table with a bottle of red wine. Clint checked it out and nodded his approval. "I took the liberty of ordering for both of us," he told me. "Needless to say, we're having steak. And this Pinot Noir is from a fine local winery. I believe you'll enjoy it."

I tasted the wine. "Oh my, yes," I said. "This is delicious."

He smiled. "Glad you approve. And wait until you sample our beef." He sat back and took a long, slow taste of his wine.

"Can we talk some more about changes you've made to eliminate the rustling?" I asked him. Despite the lovely wine, this was, after all, still a business dinner.

"I'd actually prefer that you discuss those details with Jess Parker. He's in charge of the ranching operations. He'll be able to give you a far more detailed summary of what we've done. I can set up a meeting for you with him. How about tomorrow morning?"

"Could we make that tomorrow afternoon instead? I asked. "I need to have a talk with the local police in the morning."

"Not a problem. I can text you the details tomorrow. Texting's not my favorite trick, but it certainly can be efficient at times."

That made me smile. Perhaps I had met a fellow technophobe.

Clint raised his glass in toast. "So, like I was saying earlier, I sure do regret the sorry welcome you got when you arrived this morning. Let's see what we can do to make up for that from here on."

I sipped my wine. "Don't worry about a thing. It was obvious you had far more pressing things on your mind. Such a horrible way for that poor fellow to die."

"A tragic accident. That's for sure. We're trying to deal with it quietly and discreetly so as not to upset our guests. It's not an easy thing to do. Gus was well-liked around here. Just an all-round good guy. Not to mention a valued employee. He will be missed." Clint lowered his eyes and shook his head slowly. "Anyway, like I said, I know you're here to do a job, but there's no need to get all tangled up with all work and no play."

"Thanks." I searched for the right words to describe my first impression of the inn. "This certainly is quite a place."

Clint smiled. "We're proud of it. We have a lot to offer our guests. I sure hope you'll be able to take advantage of some of our amenities and activities while you're here. There's the spa and the pool, of course. Also a fitness center. Games are available in the garden - corn hole, tennis and basketball. We provide tennis lessons as well."

I had seen those on my walk earlier. The tennis and basketball courts were bright pink.

"We've also got some wonderful hiking trails," Clint continued. "There are bicycles available for rental. And horseback riding. That's always popular."

"I'd be particularly interested in riding the trails to check out the area where the rustling has been occurring. That would combine business with a bit of fun."

"That'd be great. Back in college, I rode fairly regularly. It's been a while, but I'd love to give it a try. It would be a great way to get the lay of the land here and see where the cattle have gone missing."

"I will arrange that for you, complete with a personal guide," he said.

Perhaps that guide could be Lance? I chose not to vocalize that thought.

"What else can I tell you about?"

I asked him something which had been on my mind since I first reviewed the claim. "There is one thing I've been wondering about. You have both an inn and a cattle ranch here. That's an unusual combination. What's the connection?"

"There is none," Clint laughed. "It's all about history. You see, there have been cattle ranches in this part of California since way back, long before it was even a state. Mr. Madonna decided to continue that tradition when he purchased the property in the 1950s. It used to be a much larger operation. At one time, there were three partners involved, Mr. Madonna, a fellow named Louis Johnson and, believe it or not, John Wayne."

"*The* John Wayne?"

"Yes, Ma'am."

I made a note about that. This was information that probably wouldn't make it into the computer file, but perhaps Peggy could find a way to work it in. It was always good to add something of interest.

"In those days," Clint continued, "there were over several thousand head of cattle here. The operation's much smaller these days. Now we only raise enough cattle for our own needs. And we still do it the old way, the right way. Our cows are grass-fed and hormone-free. That's a big deal these days, you know. The quality of our steaks is critical to our success. We're not about to go messing with a sure thing."

Our meals arrived. Clint was right about the steak. Delicious didn't begin to describe it.

"Anything else you need," Clint said, "anybody you want to talk to, just let me know. Jess can help you with that as well. We're all here to help you settle this claim any way we can. And we'll be working hard at solving this rustling problem as well. Got to put a stop to that before it puts us out of business.".

"I'll drink to that," I said. "And by the way, everybody I have met here so far has been just wonderful – friendly, helpful. You should be proud of your employees."

That brought a smile to Clint's face. "Good to hear. Anybody in particular I should know about? So I can give them a pat on the back the next time I see them?"

That was easy. "Both Steve in the office and Rosa in the café were particularly nice, and very helpful. I also met an interesting fellow named Lance. He was pleasant as well." *Pleasant and then some!* "He was working with an older may. Rather short. Thick white hair. Didn't say much."

"That'd be Pickins. Now there's a fellow you should get to know. He'd be a great source of information about both the inn and the ranch. He's been working here forever. Way longer than me."

I made a mental note to spend some time with Pickins. "Lance offered to help me as well, in any way he could."

"Lance said that, huh?" Clint chuckled at that, but held his tongue. It made me wonder what he knew about Lance that I didn't. And how I could find out what it was.

Clint and I shared a lovely piece of pecan pie for dessert, then said good-night. As much as I appreciated both Clint's company and the information he was providing for my investigation, I was happy to make it an early evening. My day had already been three hours longer than usual. I'd be happy to call it a night.

AVENGING MADONNA

My phone dinged as I was getting ready for bed. I had a text message. I didn't recognize the number, but opened it anyway – something for which Peggy would surely scold me. The message read "Sorry things got busy at the restaurant and we didn't get a chance to continue our conversation. I'm sure we'll get another opportunity real soon. In the meantime, sure hope you're settling in. See you soon. – Rosa" My initial reaction was: *How nice of her.* Then something else occurred to me: *How the devil did the girl get my cell number?*

Chapter 8

I was awake and out of bed early the next morning. It seemed that my body was still on Boston time. The trouble was, it was 5:00 AM where I was. My first conscious act was to call Pete. No sense putting it off any longer. My recent feelings about our relationship had left me in an uneasy state of mind. I needed to face my feelings and sort them out, not run away from them. I dreaded doing so.

"Good morning, Ames. I'm so glad you called," he said. "Sorry I missed your call yesterday. Court went on far longer than expected. It ended up taking my entire day. Then as long as I was in the Boston area, I stopped by Peggy's to say hello to Sam. He and I had a nice long walk and a good chat. He's fine, but I know he misses you almost as much as I do."

"I'm sure he was thrilled to see you."

"Right. It made for a long day, but it was worth it. However, it also put me behind with other stuff at the office. I've got to take care of that today."

What about last evening? Any reason you didn't call me then?

Pete answered that question before I had a chance to ask it. "I was planning to connect with you in the evening, but I got side-tracked."

"Oh? By what? It must have been something very important." I was pretty sure he'd know that I was teasing.

He laughed. "As a matter of fact, it might be important to you. I started watching an old movie while I ate a late dinner. Got so involved in it I couldn't tear myself away."

That wasn't exactly what I expected to hear. "So you're saying that an old movie took priority over me?"

"No," he said. "I watched it because of you. It was connected to your investigation."

"How so?"

"It was an old western, about cattle rustling. I thought I might learn something that could help your case."

Interesting. "Okay. Tell me about it."

"The movie was called "The Moonlighter." It's from 1953 and stars Fred MacMurray and Barbara Stanwyck. Ward Bond was in it as well."

"Of course he was," I said. "Wasn't he in all the old westerns?"

Pete laughed. "Right, though this time he was a bad guy."

"That's a switch. But, tell me, if it's a movie about cattle rustling, why is it called The Moonlighter?"

"That's what I thought might help your case. You see, a moonlighter is what they called a particular type of cattle rustler. He's a guy who's an expert with a lasso. He works only at night, and by the light of the moon. This moonlighter sneaks onto the grazing land, identifies a few cows without the usual herd mentality."

"Are you saying there are alpha steers?"

Pete laughed. "So it would seem. Apparently there are some who tend to graze apart from the rest of the herd. The moonlighter ropes these animals and hauls them into his truck. The other steers follow meekly behind. And this moonlighter takes off with the entire herd."

"That is all very interesting. And it sounds like a pretty good movie. But tell me, please, how does this tie in to settling my claim?

The folks here aren't losing their entire herd. It's more like a steer or two every now and then."

"Perhaps you're dealing with the modern version of moonlighters. The sneakier kind, who think nobody will notice a missing cow or two here and there, at least not until they've absconded with a bunch of them. Anyway, it's more about identifying the perps," he told me.

"Which is something I would very much like to do," I said. "Not to mention arresting the lot of them."

"Look for the guys who are expert ropers. The timing of the thefts is a factor as well. These rustlers work on moon-lit nights. That's when the ranchers need to be on their guard. And the local sheriff needs to be on alert."

The bit about the moon might be useful. I wasn't sure the rest of the information was, but I did appreciate Pete's efforts. Perhaps it would somehow help with my investigation. Or at least make me sound more knowledgeable to the folks at the ranch. "That's good to know," I said. "Thanks for the info."

"Turns out the movie was less about rustling and more about what happens to the rustler after he escapes from jail before they get around to hanging him, but by the time I realized that, I was really involved in the story. It was quite well done. And then it was too late to call you."

He added this last part meekly, like he was trying to convince himself. Or perhaps he didn't quite get the three-hour time difference. Whatever. I decided to let that slide and move on.

So, tell me what I'm missing in California," he continued. "Any more rustling?"

I described the Madonna Inn in detail, then filled him in on what little I had done or learned so far, as well as the recent death of the cowhand. I included the history of the Lion's Den but did not, however, mention my new friend Lance. I saw no point in stirring up that pot, at least not yet.

"Sounds like quite a place," Pete said. "I'm sorry I won't get to see it."

"Aren't you planning on flying out here in a day or so?" I asked him. Then I almost wished I hadn't.

"The way things are shaping up at work, probably not. Believe me, Ames, I really want to join you, but I'm simply in no position to be away from the office right now. I'm so sorry."

I wasn't quite sure if I was sorry or not, but decided to take the kinder, gentler route. "It's all right Pete. Don't worry about it. I'll be pretty busy with my investigation anyway. I probably wouldn't have a lot of time for you."

He let out a sigh. "Thank you for being so understanding. That's why I love you so much. I'll make it up to you real soon. I promise."

"That's fine. And I will hold you to that promise," I said. "I better let you go now. We both have busy days ahead of us." And no matter how my day played out, I was pretty sure it'd be more interesting than Pete's day in his office. And I was eager to see how.

Chapter 9

My first official mission of the day was a visit to the San Luis Obispo police station. It was a short visit. I was greeted by a middle-aged Hispanic woman in a crisp blue uniform. She had wavy black hair and a scowl on her face.

"Good morning," I said as I handed her my card. "I need to speak with someone about the recent rustling issues at the Madonna Ranch."

The look on her face screamed "What are you, new here?" She actually said, "Sorry, we can't help you. You'll need to speak with the agricultural agent at the county sheriff's office. Rustling is their bailiwick."

I would have liked to stick around a little longer and ask the police about the death of the Madonna ranch hand, just in case it was connected to my investigation. There was no point in trying, though. The police wouldn't give me any information because I wasn't officially involved. At least not yet.

Luckily, it was a short walk to the sheriff's office. Also a lovely morning for such a walk. A slightly overweight older fellow with a bushy white mustache and eyebrows to match sat at a desk in the lobby. His badge identified him as Henry Ellis. "Morning Ma'am," he said. "What can we do for you this lovely day?"

I handed him my card. "I need to speak with somebody about the recent rustling activity at the Madonna Ranch. I'm investigating the loss for their insurance company."

"Sure thing," he said. "That'd be Walt Benson you'll be wanting to speak with. He's the AG here."

"AG?" I asked. *Did this county have an attorney general?*

"That's the agricultural agent in the Rural Crime Unit. He deals with everything related to theft or property damage in the local rural communities. I'll give him a call."

Henry picked up the phone. "Hey, Walt. There's a young lady here looking to talk with you about the recent rustling incidents at the Madonna Ranch." He listened for a moment. "Yeah. Okay. Will do." Turning to me, he said, "Go down that hallway on the right. Walt's office is the second on the left. He'll be waiting for you."

"Thank you." And off I went, pleased that Henry Ellis thought I was a lady, not to mention young.

Walt Benson greeted me in the hallway with a big smile. One of his front teeth was missing. He was short and sinewy, with large brown eyes and most likely Mexican blood. "Come on in, Ma'am. Make yourself comfortable and tell me what I can do for you today."

I sat in the chair facing his cluttered desk and handed him my card. He barely glanced at it. The wall behind Walt was cluttered with framed photos and plaques, all honoring him in one way or another. Not to mention displaying his missing tooth. If these were any indication, he was a popular guy in San Luis Obispo County. I hoped it was because he was so good at his job. That would be helpful to me. Pulling out my notebook and pen, I began, "I'm investigating the recent rustling incidents at the Madonna Ranch. I'd appreciate anything you can tell me."

He put his feet up on his desk and leaned back in his chair. "Sure thing. Where'd you like to start?"

"How about we begin with rustling in general?" I suggested. "This is my first claim of this nature. I was actually surprised to learn that this sort of crime still happens. I always associated rustling with the old west."

Walt nodded. "And rightly so. Cattle thieving was a major problem back in the bad old days. Far worse than it is now. And it was often settled by vigilante justice. You know, hang 'em now. Ask questions later - but only if you have the time. I'm happy to say that doesn't happen anymore."

I couldn't argue with that, particularly the part about asking questions only if you had the time. "How common is rustling nowadays?" I asked.

"That depends. It gets to be more of a problem whenever beef prices rise. After all, it's a crime of low risk and high reward. When done well, it can be an easy way for a fellow to make some fast cash."

"What I don't understand is how anybody can get away with it," I said. "After all, aren't all cattle branded?"

Walt shook his head. "Not so much anymore. Most ranchers have given it up entirely."

"Why is that?"

He stared up at the ceiling, as if deep in thought. "Fact is that branding's no real solution, for a number of reasons."

"Like what?"

"First of all, calves aren't usually branded until they're at least 60 days old. If they're stolen before that, there's just no way of ever identifying who owns any of them."

That made some sense to me. "But what about afterwards?" I asked. "Once a calf has been branded? Wouldn't it be easy to identify them then?"

"Not always. Brands can be altered, you know. It's a whole lot easier than you'd think. The rustlers just have to come up with a logo that can be superimposed over the old brand and make it look like something else entirely. Could be something as simple as turning a Y into an X. It happens all the time. And there's no real way to prove it once it's been done."

I hadn't thought of that. I had to admit it was clever.

"And that's not all," Walt continued. "There's lots of ranchers out there who simply choose not to brand their cattle, particularly if they're looking to sell the hides."

I tossed that thought around in my brain. "Does branding an animal somehow change the value of a hide?"

He gave me a big, semi-toothless smile. "Good for you. That's it exactly. You see, in the leather business, a brand is considered a flaw in the hide. It makes that piece unusable. This can have a big, and bad, effect on the selling price."

"So it's basically a case of damned if you do and damned if you don't," I said.

"That's for sure. What else can I tell you?"

I gave that some thought. "Exactly how are cattle rustled these days?"

"There are a couple of different ways," Walt said. "The easiest way is by what I like to call cheating. That happens when a cow strays onto a neighbor's property. The neighbor simply holds onto the animal for a while. Breeds her. Once she produces a calf or two, he lets her go. The cow mysteriously shows up back on the owner's land a year or two later. That sort of thing is hard to prove as well. Anybody could claim it's nothing more than a case of a lost cow finding her way back home."

"Does that happen often?" I asked.

Walt shrugged. "Who knows? There's no real way to tell."

I could see what he meant. "What is the most common method of rustling?"

"Just steal the cattle outright. There's acres and acres of hills and valleys out there, all pretty secluded. All a thief has got to do is park his truck somewhere out of sight in the hills and lure the critters into it."

"How do you lure them in?"

"It's a lot easier than you'd think," he said. "Just spread a little hay in front of the critters and you can lead them pretty much anywhere you want."

"That sounds almost too easy."

"It is," he agreed, "so long as you don't get caught."

I thought back to my conversation with Pete this morning. Got to put a stop to that before it puts us out of business. "Is that what's called moonlighting?"

That got a laugh from Walt. "Where'd you hear that term?"

"From a friend. He saw it in an old movie."

"With Barbara Stanwyck and Fred MacMurray," Walt said.

"And Ward Bond," I added.

He smiled. "I've seen that movie myself, more than once. And you're right about moonlighting. It's a type of rustling limited to moonlit nights. It's also limited to thieves who are talented with a rope. And once again, all you have to do is park your truck nearby and away you go, with a whole lot of somebody else's cattle."

"How do you police something like that?" I asked. "It has to be tricky if all of this is happening at night."

"That's for sure. Nighttime makes it tough. During the day, we do a fair amount of aerial surveillance. Looking for unattended or suspicious vehicles parked near grazing areas. Then we follow up on them when darkness hits. The trouble is that the farther out in the hills these grazing areas are, the tougher our job becomes."

"What happens if you do catch the thieves? Assuming you're not hanging them anymore, that is."

Walt laughed. "Some people would still like to. That's for darn sure. The penalties for being caught rustling are kind of stiff though. Usually 20 years in prison and a $20,000 fine."

"That ought to be enough to discourage people," I said.

"You'd think so, wouldn't you?"

I read over the notes I had taken during my conversation with Clint, then said to Walt, "From what you're telling me, it seems to me that several head of cattle are usually stolen at the same time."

He nodded. "Right. A body might as well make the most of the opportunity."

"But that's not what's happening at the Madonna Ranch. They're losing only one or two cows at a time."

Walt furrowed his brow. "You're right about that. And it doesn't make much sense – at least from the rustler's point of view."

"And then there are the cows that have simply been killed and left there."

"I can't explain that either," he said, shaking his head. "Any rustler worth his salt would take even a dead cow. There's still some value to be had with them. It'd be crazy to leave them in the hills."

And yet that was exactly what was happening, at least at the Madonna Ranch. I spent a few moments mulling over everything I'd just heard. "If I understand you correctly, you are not having much luck yet tracking down the cattle taken from the Madonna Ranch."

"Nope. And that's a darn shame."

A darn shame and then some. "Have you seen much rustling lately in and around San Luis Obispo County other than at the Madonna Ranch?" I asked.

He took a moment to give that some thought. "Now that you mention it, I don't believe I have."

"Why do you suppose that is?"

Walt shrugged. "Damned if I know. It's kind of funny, though, isn't it?"

Not so funny for the Madonna Ranch, or for NEC&I. "Can you give me any specifics on how your investigation will proceed from here?"

That question seemed to stump him. "I'm going to have to think about that, Ma'am. We do the best we can, you know. The sad truth is that sometimes it just doesn't work out like we want. That doesn't mean we won't keep trying, though. I'll let you know if anything else comes up." He held up my card as if to confirm he knew how to reach me.

I frowned as I thought about what he had said. I also wondered how much time my friend here spent doing his job, and how much he spent posing for pictures. NEC&I would pay the claim of course. And happily so. That was our job. But so was working with our clients to prevent similar losses in the future. Besides, I really wanted to find the missing cattle and identify the guilty party. That was often the most satisfying part of my job. Not to mention the most fun. And I wasn't about to give up on it yet. I could afford to spend a few extra days in San Luis Obispo to see what I could discover.

Chapter 10

I decided to forego lunch completely and have an early dinner instead. Forgoing a meal was definitely not my usual MO, but today it made sense. It gave me the time to make some notes for my 1:00 meeting with Jess Parker, the foreman of the ranching operation. I was eager to question him on a number of things, mostly concerning ranching, rustling and personnel. It was a lovely day for a stroll, sunny with a refreshing breeze. I walked the narrow road behind the inn, following the signs for Trail Rides. White horse fences like I'd seen in Kentucky lined both sides of the road. Horses grazed nearby in groups of two or three. All totally bucolic.

I headed for a barnboard cabin sporting a wooden sign which read Happy Trails. A fellow in faded jeans, well-worn boots and a dusty cowboy hat was standing in the open doorway gazing off into the horizon. He was lanky and tanned, probably in his mid-to-late-fifties.

"Howdy, Ma'am," he greeted me. "I'd be guessing you must be Ms. Lynch."

"You'd be correct." I shook his hand. "It's a pleasure to meet you. And please call me Amy."

"The pleasure is all mine, Amy," he replied. He indicated two wooden rocking chairs on the porch of the cabin. "Come on over here and have a seat. No sense spending such a beautiful day closed up inside the office."

He was right about that. I sat, gave him a big smile and pulled out my notes. "I appreciate you taking the time to meet with me. I don't know much about cattle ranching, or rustling. I have a lot of questions."

"Not a problem," he said. "I'm happy to be of service. We need to put all this trouble to an end. Fast. So, what can I tell you?"

"Let's begin with the basics. How many people does it take to run a cattle ranch like this?"

"Up until recently, we usually had seven ranch hands."

"Clint told me you have about 150 head of cattle. Is seven the average number of cowboys for a ranch of this size?"

He shook his head. "In general, no. Most ranches get by with four or five hands. We need more here because our guys are more than simply cowboys."

"What do you mean?"

He rocked back in his chair, then said, "Well, first of all there's the regular ranching work - fencing, irrigating, moving the cattle around, doctoring them when they need it, helping to birth the calves, branding – but there's a lot more that needs doing around here."

"Because of the inn?" I asked.

"Exactly. Because the Madonna properties are both a ranch and an inn, the hands are also responsible for most of the maintenance work at the inn – landscaping, painting, minor repairs and the like. And they guide guests on trail rides. That's a big part of their jobs during the busy season."

I let all that sink in. "That's a pretty full job description. And seven ranch hands can handle all that? It sounds like you keep them pretty busy."

"That's a fact," Jess said. "There's no sense at all in paying a fellow just to hang around being idle. We did just fine with seven of them up until recently. We added two more when the rustling problems started."

"May I have the names of your current ranch hands?" I asked. Maybe that wasn't actually necessary, but you never know. It wouldn't hurt to have Peggy do a thorough background check on them.

"Sure thing. There's Pickins and Rusty Daniels. Both of them have been here for years. Both were here when I was hired. And that was longer ago than I care to admit. Salt of the earth, these fellas. Don't know what I'd do without them."

I put them on my list.

"Then there's the younger fellas," Jess continued. "Lance, Don, Brody, and Frank. Also Gus. Lord rest his poor soul. These guys have all been here for a couple of years or so."

I'd met Lance, and heard about the late Gus. The others were new to me.

"Could you provide me with their last names? It may not matter in the end, but I do like to be thorough."

"Not a problem," Jess replied. "I was thinking you'd be needing them." He handed me a list of names, first and last.

"This is great. Thanks." I looked the list over and added it to my notes. "And what is the role of these additional men?"

Jess nodded. "We hired them when we started up the night shift. Guys named Arty and Juan. Neither of them worked out so well. Arty drank too much. And Juan was downright lazy. Had to let them both go. We were back to seven, and working them hard. Then we lost Gus."

I'd deal with that issue shortly. Once I'd covered all bases on the rustling problem. After all, that was my primary purpose here. "Are you looking now to hire a few more hands?" I asked.

"Got to. We need the extra help to man the night shift. And we need to have that until this damn rustling stops once and for all."

"How long have you been running a night shift?"

"Going on two, three months now. Started it up as soon as we realized what was going on. Couldn't afford not to," he said.

"How many men work this shift?"

"Two," he said.

"I'm guessing that the two of them work together rather than splitting up out in the hills."

"They sure do. It gets dark in those hills at night. There's lots of ways a fellow could get hurt. Safer for folks to be working together."

"Is it always the same two people?" I asked.

"Nope. I rotate all the hands, so everybody does some time out there at night. And I've started keeping track of who's been working where when a steer goes missing. I'm hoping I might pick up some interesting insights from that."

I made a few notes, feeling good about what I had learned so far. "Please tell me about the safety measures they take in the hills at night. Like lanterns or cell phones."

"Everybody uses both," Jess said. "They also have flashlights, big ones, as a back-up. You know, just in case something goes wrong with a lantern."

This all sounded good so far.

"I thought I'd work that shift myself off and on too," Jess continued. "So I can see first-hand what's going on. Being out there in the hills at night, perhaps I'll find a way to figure out what's been happening. Maybe even catch the damn thieves in the act. Gotta stop these bastards somehow. And the night shift's a good start."

"What else are you doing to prevent further rustling problems?" I asked. This was critical. It could determine whether or not NEC&I would keep the Madonna Ranch on as a client. If the rustling continued, that would be a losing proposition.

"Besides the night shift, we're also starting to do a head count every couple of days for a while, instead of just once every month or so. It'll create more work for everyone, but it should be worth the effort. We definitely can't let things go on the way they are."

It was good to know the man had a plan. It'd be interesting in seeing how that all played out. "Well let's hope these extra measures help," I said. "And that the rustling or killing of your stock comes to an end." *Or you folks may end up having to find a new insurance company. And we'd hate to see that happen.*

"Amen to that," he said. He closed his eyes as if in deep thought. Finally he said, "Thinking about it now, I wonder if I should have hired a few more hands sooner. Maybe then things would've been different for Gus."

"That was such a shame," I said. "Such a horrible way to die."

Jess gazed off into the distance. "That's for sure. Damn pity, too. Gus did a fine job. Really knew what he was doing. Got along great with folks. I sure am gonna miss him around here."

"Please tell me what happened the night Gus died," I said. Perhaps it wasn't technically connected to my case, but it couldn't hurt to know the details, just in case. I didn't mention anything else I'd already heard. Better to see what Jess would have to say about it, and what he might add, or leave out.

Jess frowned. "Gus hated doing the night shift. Made no bones about it either. But there was nothing I could do about that. Everybody had to take his turn. And that was that." Jess fell silent.

I waited to see what else he might have to say.

"Brody was supposed to be working with Gus that night, like he usually did," Jess added. "Never showed up though. Claims he called in sick. Had some sort of stomach bug. Says he left a message. I never got it, though. Nothing at all on the answering machine. Don't quite know how that happened."

"Answering machine?" I asked. "Not a voicemail on your cell phone?"

Jess shrugged. "Answering machine in the office has been working just fine for us for ages now. No point in changing something that ain't broke."

Or perhaps it was actually broken. "Are you certain the machine was on that day?" I asked.

Jess nodded. "Sure was. Always is. I've had a few new messages left on it since then, so I know it's working just fine."

"What do you think happened? With Brody, I mean."

"One of two things," Jess replied. "Either something went wrong with the machine, which I doubt, or Brody's lying. I don't know which for sure, but I have my suspicions. Not really sure I want to know the details. It doesn't make much difference now. Gus is gone and that's a fact."

That took me by surprise. "Are you saying you don't want to know if Brody lied to you?"

"Not right now. Too much else going on at the moment. Stuff that's more important. I'll deal with Brody. Make no mistake about that. But I'll do it in my own time. And in my own way." The look on his face added "so there" without actually saying it out loud.

"Would it be a problem for you if I questioned Brody?" I intended to do it anyway, but I wanted to see how Jess felt about it.

"No," he told me. "Not at all. You've got a job to do here. Talking to Brody is part of it. Today's his day off, though. Gotta give them all one day off a week no matter what. Or there'd be nobody willing to work here. Brody'll be in tomorrow morning. You can come back and see him then."

That sounded like a plan. "So what happened with Gus? Did he have a cell phone with him? Did he call for someone else to work with him when Brody didn't show up?"

"That's a good question. Nobody's found his phone, not on his body, not in either the ravine or the bunk house. Darn thing just went missing somehow. And that's a worry. I keep hoping it'll turn up somewhere."

"What about lights? Did Gus have both a lantern and a flashlight like he was supposed to?"

"His lantern was in the barn. Don't know why he didn't take it with him. It makes no damn sense. He never should've gone into the hills without it. Had his flashlight with him, sure enough, but the battery was dead. That's hard to explain. Gus was way too smart to let something like that happen. He always changed the flashlight battery every day or two, just to be sure."

I thought long and hard for a bit, then decided I had to say, "Does it strike you as something more than a coincidence that all these things happened the same night? Brody didn't show up. Gus didn't have the lantern with him. The flashlight died. Are you sure what happened to Gus was an accident?"

Jess closed his eyes and grimaced as if in pain. "I've been thinking the same thing myself. Just can't decide what to do about it, though. Not yet, anyway. Gotta wait and see what the police have to say. And the coroner. Gotta stop the rustling too. When all of that's taken care of, then I'll think about the rest. But don't you go worrying none, Ma'am. These things tend to have a way of working out right in the end, just the way they're supposed to. A body simply needs the patience to let fate do its thing. It'll all come out just fine."

I had some trouble buying that, but decided not to say so. I'd bide my time as well for now. And see what developed. In the meantime, I had a few more questions for Jess.

"Do you have any thoughts on who these rustlers might be?" I asked.

"Wish I did. Sorry."

"Do you think anybody working here might be involved?"

Jess gave me a horrified look. "I'm trying hard not to go down that road. At least not yet."

I had one final question for Jess. And it went back to something Rosa in the restaurant had said. "Do you allow beer or other liquor out here? For the ranch hands when they're off duty?"

"Hell no. No Ma'am. Never." Jess almost shouted these words. "If these folks want to drink, they're gonna have to go into town for that. Alcohol is the tool of the devil. No way it's ever allowed on the ranch. I've seen too much bad come from drinking in my time. We can't have that start happening here."

"Has that always been the rule?" I asked.

"You bet. My father was a drunk, you see. Damn near killed my mother and destroyed our family. I've never touched the stuff myself. Never will."

Funny, I could have sworn Rosa told me Jess had a drinking problem. One of them was lying to me. But who?

Chapter 11

Before I could ponder that question, I spotted a fellow storming toward us with fire in his eyes. He was short, with sun-worn skin and a thick patch of white hair seriously in need of a trim. I wasn't sure, but he looked like the older fellow I had seen yesterday working with Lance.

"Uh oh," Jess said. "Here comes Pickins. And from the look on his face, I'm guessing he's armed for bear. Something must have pissed the guy off big time. Oops, excuse me, Ma'am. Pardon the language."

"Not a problem. What do you suppose he's so worked up about?" I asked.

Jess shrugged. "Sure looks like we're about to find out." He stood as Pickins approached us on the porch. "Afternoon, Pick. How're you doing today?"

"I'm mad as hell," Pickins snarled. "And if I ever catch up with the son of a bitch, I'm going to give him what for."

I wasn't quite sure what 'what for' might entail, but my guess was it wouldn't be anything pleasant.

Jess put his hands on his hips. "And exactly which son of a bitch would that be?"

"That damn Huddleston, that's who." Pickins spat out. "I'm gonna kill the dude next time I see him. Seems like young kids these days do whatever they damn please. And they don't give a gopher's ass about anybody they might inconvenience in the process."

They probably didn't give a hoot either.

"So just what did Don do to get you so riled up?" Jess asked. "Do I need to have a little talk with the guy?"

"Only if you can find him," Pickins replied.

Jess gave him a confused look. "What the hell are you talking about? Is he missing or something?"

"Worse than that," Pickins growled. "He's gone."

"What do you mean gone? Is he taking the afternoon off without telling anybody?"

"More like taking the rest of his life off. At least from here."

"What the heck does that mean?" Jess asked.

"This is what it means." Pickins shoved a folded paper toward Jess. "He left this note on his bunk."

Jess unfolded the note, read for a moment, then scowled. "I see what you mean." He turned to me. "Don's note says he's leaving. Quitting as of right now. No explanation. No notice. Just quitting. Gone."

"Who the hell does he think he is to up and leave like that?" Pickins growled. "The decent thing for him to do would be to give a little notice. So we could find a replacement for him."

"Maybe not," Jess said. "Once a body's made his mind up to go, there's not much sense in keeping him around, even for a little while. Lord knows what kind of mischief a person could get into once he doesn't care anymore."

Pickins scowled at that idea.

I thought Jess had a good point.

"Not only did he just take off like that," Pickins continued, "but he left one hell of a mess behind."

"A mess of what?" Jess asked.

"Pretty much all of his worldly possession, from the looks of things," Pickins growled. "Now I'm stuck having to clean it up. Like I've got nothing better to do with my time." The look in his eyes suggested he might be getting ready to explode again.

Jess spoke up just in time. "I'll see if I can get one of the other guys to give you a hand with that."

Pickins almost smiled. "That'd be good. Thanks."

"And in the meantime, how about you calm yourself down a mite? Join me and this lovely lady here on the porch?"

Pickins sat down on the porch steps. He looked at me as if he had only just noticed my presence. "Didn't I see you the other day?" he asked me. "Talking to Lance down by the Lion's Den."

"That's right," I said.

He grinned. "Shouldn't be telling you this, but Lance has been looking around for you ever since. Like he's hoping maybe you'll come by and spend a little time with him, if you know what I mean."

I knew what he meant. I had been hoping the same thing, though trying my darnedest not to admit it, not even to myself.

"Meet Amy Lynch," Jess told him. "Amy, this is Pickins. He's one of our most experienced ranch hands. Been with us for ages."

"Howdy, Ma'am," Pickins said. "I'm sorry you had to witness that little tantrum just now. I really do know how to behave in front of a lady, you know. It's just that sometimes my temper gets the better of me. Anyway, I'm happy to make your acquaintance."

Jess continued, "Amy is from the insurance company. She's here to look into our rustling claim. I'm hoping you'll have some time tomorrow to take her riding in the hills. Show her around some."

"I'd especially like to see the grazing areas of the property," I said. "To get a good idea of where the cattle spend their time, where they are before they go missing, as well as where the dead ones have been found."

"Right," Pickins said, visibly calmer now. "It'd be my pleasure. Would afternoon be all right with you? We're doing a head count around noon time. It'll be right here at the ranch. I imagine you'll want to join us for that. We could ride out in the hills right after. That would give us time to have a good look around and be back in plenty of time for supper.

"That would be great," I told him. I was pleased to hear about the upcoming head count. It would be interesting to see how it was done, not to mention learning the results.

Jess added, "Thanks for that, Pick. We all need to do what we can to help Amy, so we can get this darn claim paid, stop the rustling and the killing and get back to the business of raising cattle."

Pickins nodded. "That's for damn sure." He shook his head. "Raising cattle's what we're here to do, not cleaning up each other's messes in the bunk house. Damn that Huddleston. In the end, I'll probably end up throwing everything out. Most of it is just plain old junk anyway."

Jess jumped in before Pickins could go ballistic again. "Now don't you go worrying about that. Like I said, I'll get you some help."

Pickins furrowed his brow. "One thing I sure don't get is why the guy left his notes. You know, for that damn book he claimed to be writing. Why do you suppose he'd want to leave those? For a guy who was always acting like he was smarter than the rest of us, and bragging about being a writer, leaving all his notes behind – 'research' he called it – that's just plain odd. Makes no damn sense to me."

Jess spoke up before I got a chance to speak. "Notes? Book? What the hell are you talking about now?"

I set my questions aside for a moment to hear more about this book.

"Don claimed to be some kind of historian," Pickins said. "And a writer to boot. Said he was working on a book about the local history here. You know, telling how things were back in the bad old days. He was always poking around, asking folks all kinds of questions. Mostly bugging people that he knew grew up around here. They didn't like it much. Thought he was a bit too nosy. I tended to agree."

As intriguing as that book sounded, I had more important matters to pursue at the moment – mostly concerned with sorting out my claim. And Don might just figure into it. "You know, you're right. It doesn't make much sense for this guy to take off and leave his so-called research behind like that. There has got to be something else going on here."

"Like what?" Pickins asked.

Jess turned to face me. "Are you thinking what I'm thinking?"

"Possibly," I replied.

Pickins looked from Jess to me and back to Jess again. "Anybody going to tell me what the two of you are thinking?"

I answered for the both of us. "Do you think Don may be somehow involved in the rustling?"

Jess shrugged. Pickins' eyes grew wide.

I held my tongue. I didn't know what I thought yet. I added looking into Don Huddleston's disappearance to my "to do" list. And I needed to do it right away.

Chapter 12

It was nearly 4:00 when I returned from the ranch. I decided to
kill a little time before dinner checking out the infamous men's
room, then visit the gift shop, hoping to find a special gift for
Pete. Something that might help to chase away my recent doubts
about him as well as my thoughts about Lance. My conscience would
appreciate the effort. I headed into the main building where the
restroom in question was located, along with a few shops and the two
restaurants.

The way to the men's' room was well marked - downstairs and
to the left. An older fellow seated outside the door informed me that
the coast was clear. The rest room was not in use at the moment. He
was wearing an employee name tag. I wondered if monitoring the use
of this particular men's room was part of his job. Or perhaps all of it?
I was pretty sure the Inn wouldn't want to be upsetting the gentlemen
guests while they were using the facilities.

I passed two middle-aged women on my way in. They giggled
as they held the door for me. Perhaps this was their first visit to a
men's room. Perhaps the famous urinal was every bit as entertaining
as the rumors claimed. One of the women lowered her voice and
informed me, "The waterfall starts up when someone pees."

Good to know.

Once inside, I took a look around. It was definitely not a case of "If you've seen one urinal, you've seen them all." This particular fixture occupied the best part of one entire wall. It was tall and wide, built of what appeared to be stone. There was no water running down it at the moment. I guessed that nobody had peed recently. It still made me smile. I snapped a picture.

OK, this is cute and clever. Time to move on now.

A gift shop occupied the rest of the lower floor. It was quiet at the moment, only a clerk and two teenage girls inside. I took a quick stroll around. Madonna Inn tee shirts, mugs and baseball caps. Other assorted souvenirs, mostly of the standard variety. Also an area for wine tasting, which was not currently in use. The merchandise was all nice enough, but I had something else in mind for Pete. Something really nice. I did, however, grab a couple bottles of local wine – a Sauvignon Blanc and a Pinot Noir – to keep in my room. It would be good to have something to sip on while I worked in the evening. I also picked up a book on the history of San Luis Obispo County. It would give me something to read – far better than watching TV. From what I had heard from the people I'd met so far, I had a feeling it would be an interesting history.

The clerk, a curly-haired middle-aged woman named Alicia, was working behind the counter. She caught my eye, and seemed to read my mind. "There is another shop on the second floor," she told me. "It carries a different variety of gifts. Perhaps you'll find what you're looking for there."

I thanked her, paid for the wine and made my way to the stairs.

Alicia was right. The second-floor boutique elevated shopping to a whole new level. It displayed a variety of clothing, shoes and leather products. Everything was high quality and had no discernible connection to the Inn. I poked around for a while, looking to spot something Pete might like.

"Can I help you to find anything?" a voice from behind me asked. I turned to see what appeared to be a familiar face. A twenty-something woman emerged from the other room. She was short and solidly built, with dark eyes and lustrous black hair cut in a bob. She was wearing the white blouse and southwestern skirt which seemed to be the uniform for female employees.

My immediate reaction was, "*Rosa cut her hair.*"

"Rosa?" I asked.

The woman shook her head. "Alexa, actually."

"But you ..." I began.

She cut me off. "Yes, I know. Except for the hair, I look very much like my sister Rosa. The main reason I cut my hair was so people could tell us apart."

"And even with that, you nearly fooled me," I told her, then added, "It's nice to meet you. By the way, I'm Amy."

"Well hello, Amy," she said. "Now tell me, what can I help you find today?"

"I'm looking for a gift for my boyfriend back home. He wasn't able to join me on this trip. I'd like to find something special for him. I'm just not sure what." I was also not sure why I was providing the woman with so much superfluous information. Sometimes I actually surprised myself.

"Masculine gifts are this way," she said, indicating an area off to the right.

I followed her, checking out a few displays along the way.

"Something like this might be nice." She held up a large belt buckle. It was silver and turquoise, almost identical to the one Lance had on yesterday.

I took one look at it, then said. "Sold."

We chatted as she rang up my purchase and gift-wrapped it for me. "So you and your sister both work here," I said. "That must be nice."

She stopped wrapping long enough to unwrap a stick of gum and pop it into her mouth. "Yeah. I suppose. But the truth is we really have no choice."

"Why is that?" I was fully aware that this was none of my business, but if this woman was willing to share personal information with me, I was more than willing to listen. I was often amazed at how useful supposedly superfluous information could turn out to be.

"Rosa and I live together, a few miles outside the city limits. There are no buses in that area, and we have only one car. Not only must we work near each other, we must also have the same hours."

"That seems like a good arrangement," I said.

"We have no choice. Can't afford either a second car or an apartment in town. Rentals in San Luis Obispo are very expensive. It makes far more sense for us to live in the home where we were raised. We own it, so our only real expenses there are the property taxes and upkeep."

"You two grew up here?" I echoed.

Alexa smiled. "Right. For good or for bad, this is our hometown."

"And have you both always lived here?" I asked. *She might be familiar with the local bad guys.*

"Me, yes. I never left. Rosa left town when she married. She returned to San Luis Obispo a few years later, after her divorce."

"And moved in with you?"

"Right. And that wasn't easy at first," Alexa said. "Living together was a challenge for both of us."

The nosy investigator in me had to ask, "Why is that?"

"We were never close as kids," Alexa said. "We really didn't get along at all. We fought about pretty much everything. Or competed for it. We had to put all of that behind us, though. Because Rosa truly had no choice. She was penniless when her marriage ended. Her husband was not a nice man. He gave her nothing. And, no matter what our differences may be, I would never turn my back on my sister."

This woman really was a talker. And I was loving it. If we kept this up long enough, I was bound to learn something useful.

Something she said didn't sound right to me. "Aren't there laws in California about division of property in a divorce?"

"There are. Michael threatened to harm her if she tried to enforce them. She believed him. And simply left. Mostly out of fear."

How sad. Not to mention unfair.

"And you were able to get her a job here?"

"Yes. She was lucky the Inn was looking to hire people at that time. And she is happy enough working here. At least for now."

That statement struck me as somewhat odd. "Are you expecting that to change?"

"Yes. We both are. And it will be a change for the better." Alexa gave me a slightly creepy smile. I decided not to ask any more questions. At least for now.

Chapter 13

I decided to have dinner at the Copper Café. It would be quicker than the Gold Rush Steak House, and I didn't need a big fancy meal again tonight. Something light and healthy seemed the better choice. At least that's what I told myself. My true motive centered around Rosa. My plan was to confront her, quite nicely of course, when she wasn't overly busy yet couldn't avoid me. I needed to clarify a few issues – one of them case-related, one simply nosy.

I approached the entrance to the restaurant to see her standing in the doorway speaking with a dark-haired man who appeared to be in his early forties and in serious need of a laundromat. A shower probably wouldn't hurt him either. He was dusty and dirty and could use a shave as well.

Neither he nor Rosa saw me at first. They were too busy arguing. Rosa kept her voice low but gestured wildly with her hands. Her male opponent grasped her upper arms none too gently and shot daggers from his eyes into hers. I strained my ears, but couldn't quite pick up what they were saying.

Then they spotted me. He growled, "We'll see about that" into Rosa's face, then turned abruptly and stomped away. Rosa's cheeks reddened. She gave me what I guessed was her best phony smile. And tightened her grip on the menus in her hand. "Hello, Amy," she said. "It's nice to see you again. Table for one?"

The restaurant was busier than it had been at lunchtime the other day. About half of the tables were occupied and being served by three young waitresses. Although there were several children in the mix, the noise level was still within acceptable limits.

"How's this?" Rosa asked as we arrived at a small table by a window.

"This is fine, thanks." I sat and smiled up at her, curious to see what she would do, or say, next.

"Can I get you something to drink?" she asked.

"Sauvignon Blanc."

"Coming right up." She signaled to a waitress, passed my request on to her, then sank into the other chair at my table. "Mind if I join you?"

Actually I'd love it, particularly if you're feeling as chatty as your sister. "No problem," I told her. I definitely wanted to ask the woman a couple of questions, but decided to wait and see what she might have to say first.

Rosa fidgeted with the menus in her hands. "I hope your day went well," she began.

"Thanks. So far things are just fine," I said.

The waitress delivered my wine and took my order for a chef salad. Once she was gone, Rosa continued, "So, tell me, how is your investigation going? Did you learn anything of interest? Have you figured out what's been going on with the cattle? Or maybe heard anything new about Gus's death?"

"It's still early days," I answered. "I've got a long way to go."

"Well, I hope you're off to a good start," she said. "Did you find your way around all right? What do you think of the grounds here? Aren't they lovely?"

I nodded. "They certainly are. And on my way here just now, I checked out the famous men's room."

"Was it worth the trip?" she asked.

I nodded. "I also spent some time in both gift shops."

Rosa's eyes widened ever so slightly. Her mouth formed a small frown.

"I met your sister Alexa. She's very nice."

Rosa's gaze wandered around the restaurant as if she was looking for something. "Oh?" was all she said.

"Yes. She helped me pick out a nice gift for my boyfriend back home." I held up my bag with Pete's belt buckle in it.

Rosa gave me a tight little smile.

I continued, "Alexa and I had a nice talk while she was wrapping Pete's gift. She said that you ladies grew up right here in San Luis Obispo. And that you live together now. You two must be very close, both living and working together." I knew that I was pushing the envelope a bit here, getting too personal, but I wasn't quite sure what I thought about Rosa. I was curious to see how she would respond.

Rosa's smile faded. "Alexa says more than her prayers. She and I are quite different in that respect. I usually prefer to keep my personal life personal, and always separate from my job."

That appeared to be my cue to change the subject. "Do you have some time to answer a few questions for me?" I asked.

"About your case? Sure. What can I tell you?"

I'd love to know if there's a reason you don't want to talk about your sister. But I'll let that slide for the moment. Instead, I said, "I appreciated your text last night. That was nice of you. I am curious, though, how you came to have my cell phone number. I don't remember giving it to you." I looked her straight in the eye as I said that. There was no harm in letting her know that I noticed this type of thing.

Rosa scanned the room again. Was she trying to avoid eye contact with me?

"I got it from Steve in the office," she said. "He keeps this kind of info on file, just in case somebody needs it."

"I see." I wasn't sure why anybody other than at the front desk would need this information, but decided not to push the issue. At least not yet.

"I hope that was OK." Rosa continued. "I really enjoyed talking with you yesterday and wanted to make sure you were settled in well. We want our guests to be happy."

"That was kind of you," I told her. I didn't mention that it also seemed just a bit over the top.

"What else can I tell you?" she asked.

I didn't need to think about that. "There is one more thing," I said. "I had a talk with Jess Parker this afternoon. He made a point of letting me know that alcohol isn't allowed on the ranch. For the ranch hands, I mean."

"That's right. And it's a good idea. No sense asking for trouble, I always say. If the guys want to drink, they have to go into town."

"Jess also told me that he's a confirmed non-drinker," I continued. "But yesterday, didn't you mention to me that Jess was probably drunk when Brody called in sick that night and that was why no replacement was sent to work with Gus? Actually, I believe that what you said was 'drunk again'."

Rosa sucked in a big breath and blew it out ever so slowly. "Yes. I guess I did say that. You see, Jess used to drink. A lot. I figured he must have fallen off the wagon. Again." She glanced around the room again. "I better get back to work," she said. "Looks like somebody needs me over there."

I didn't see anybody trying to get her attention. Perhaps it was something I had said.

My chef salad arrived while I was reading over my notes from the day. I ate quickly, then returned to my room before 6:00, aka 9:00 PM Boston time. I would have loved to chat with Peggy, but it was too late for that. I'd call her at the office the first thing in the morning. I thought about calling Pete, then decided that could wait until tomorrow. There wasn't any real news at the moment. I poured myself a generous glass of wine instead. I needed to turn my thoughts off for a while and see what bubbled up on its own. I had probably already learned something useful. The question was: what?

Chapter 14

I dialed Peggy at the office as soon as I was up the next morning. "Hello to you," she greeted me. "How is life out on the range?" I gave that a moment's thought. "I've made a decent start," I told her. "I've begun interviewing people. And I'm learning a lot more about cattle ranching than I ever thought I'd want to know. It's pretty interesting, although I don't really know what I've learned yet, if you know what I mean. And I have a long way to go."

"I know exactly what you mean. You've probably already learned more than you think you have. And if you keep at it, at some point, the answer will just hit you in the face. That seems to be a pattern with you. At any rate, please tell me everything you learned so far."

I filled her in on the people I had met, as well as what I now knew about cattle ranching and cattle rustling. I made a point of including any oddball details which probably didn't matter but were definitely curious. Peggy was a master at sifting through information and culling any and all pertinent facts.

"That sounds like a good start," she said. "What about your friend Lance? What's up with him?"

I couldn't help but laugh. "Beats me. I didn't see him yesterday, which was quite all right with me." This may have been a lie.

"Yeah. Sure. But there's always tomorrow, or even later today" she reminded me. "Please keep me posted. I'd hate to miss any misadventures you may have."

"Will do. In the meantime, there is something I need you to do."

"You name it," she said.

So I did. I gave her the names of all the ranch hands, including both the recently-deceased Gus and the currently-absent Don. I added Clint and Jess to the mix as well. Might as well be thorough. "Please check these guys out for me. As thoroughly as you can. Give me anything you can find about any of them - anywhere."

"That sounds like a tall order, but I'll do my best. What sorts of things are you looking to know about them?"

"I'd be interested in anything notable, or nefarious, in their pasts. Any misdeeds or other questionable activities. You know, all the basic facts."

"Right," Peggy said. "Does this mean you suspect one or more of the ranch hands may be involved in the rustling?"

"At this point, I'm not yet sure what I believe, or even suspect. How about, for now, we say we are not yet ready to discount that possibility?"

"Gotcha. And what about that poor fellow's death? And don't tell me you haven't been looking into that as well. I know you better than that."

"Nothing to report on that. At least not yet."

Peggy laughed. "That works for me." She paused for a moment, then added, "Speaking of Lance."

I interrupted her right there. "Which we weren't."

"Well, we were a minute ago."

She was right. "OK, what about Lance?"

"It's actually more about Pete," she responded. "But talking about Lance reminded me. Pete stopped by again around the time I got home from work. He said he felt the need to visit with Sam. My gut says it's because being with Sam makes him feel closer to you."

"You're probably right." I said. "I'll bet Sam was thrilled to see him."

"I can tell he really misses you. Pete, that is, not Sam. Although I'm pretty sure Sam misses you as well."

"And I miss them both too," I told her, and that was pretty much the truth. "Please give them each a big hug for me."

"You've got it."

"Thanks," I said. "So what's going on at the office? Any juicy gossip? Major conflicts? Petty spats? Interpersonal conflicts?"

"Pretty much all of the above," was the answer.

"Explain that, please. And in great detail," I said. This was why I loved working with Peggy. She didn't miss much that went on at NEC&I. And that made my life a whole lot easier.

"Rumor has it," she began, "that George has gone to Mark to lodge a formal complaint against you."

"Went straight to the top to complain about me, huh? He's got quite a nerve. What, exactly, is the nature of his complaint this time?"

"Pretty much the same old thing," Peggy told me. "That you take all the plum cases to investigate yourself, particularly the ones that involve interesting travel. And that you leave the run-of-the-mill claims to him and his co-workers. It almost sounds as if he believes his investigating skills are comparable to yours, if not superior."

If I were totally honest, I'd admit that George might have a point there. Life is good when you can hand-pick your own assignments. But that was one of the major perks of my job, damn it. And I wasn't about to change my ways. "If his skills were all that superior," I said, "he would have been the one promoted to manager rather than me. He does realize that I'm his boss, doesn't he?" I asked.

Peggy laughed. That said it all.

"Who told you about the complaint?" I asked.

"I'm not sure I could tell you exactly who," Peggy replied. "Everybody's talking about it."

"Is Mark taking it seriously?"

"No official word on that. But I tend to doubt it."

Knowing my boss Mark as I did, I had to agree with that. "Is there anything else of interest going on?"

Peggy was silent for a moment. I could almost hear the wheels turning in her head. Finally, she replied, "No. I guess not. Sorry. So, what's on your agenda for today?"

"Ranch hands. Questioning one. Riding the range with another. Should be an interesting day. Speaking of which, I better hang up and get going. I need to meet with Brody in less than an hour." And I had high hopes for learning something interesting from him. Or perhaps catching him in a lie.

Chapter 15

I stuffed a notebook and pen into my purse. There wasn't much point in hauling my laptop around, particularly since I once again forgot to charge it. The battery was low. There were probably no electrical outlets out on the range. I plugged it in and left it to do its thing.

It was a beautiful morning, sunny with a light breeze. According to my phone, 72 degrees. Nice. As I began walking toward the ranch office, a voice behind me said, "Good morning, Ma'am. It's nice to see you again. You sure are looking lovely on this gorgeous day."

I spun around to see my new friend Lance closing the gap between us, and looking oh-so good in his cowboy attire, complete with chaps and a fringed vest. And that gorgeous belt buckle. I wondered if he selected his wardrobe to appeal to guests at the inn. "Good morning."

"Where are you off to?" he asked.

"The ranch office," I told him.

He grinned. "Funny thing, it just so happens that I'm heading that way myself. Do you mind if I join you for a bit?"

"Of course not," I said, hoping to pick up some interesting information from him along the way. At least that's what I told myself.

"We'll have to walk quickly, though. I have an 8:30 appointment and don't want to be late."

"That seems a might early in the morning to be doing business."

"I need to speak with Brody," I said. "And he starts work at 9:00."

"Brody, huh?" Lance eyed me curiously. "Good luck with that."

"Why would I need good luck?" I asked.

Lance pursed his lips. "No real reason, I guess. It's just that Brody's not known for having much to say. Mostly keeps to himself."

"Any idea why?

Lance shrugged by way of reply.

I continued. "Maybe the guy's just shy. You never know."

Lance shook his head at that suggestion. "Nope. I don't think that's it. I think he's just plain unfriendly. Also rude. To everybody. Pretty much all the time."

"That's good to know," I said. And I meant it. There was nothing I loved better than a good challenge.

We walked in silence for a while, which was fine with me. I was enjoying the exercise in the cool morning air. It also provided me some time to plan what I needed, or wanted, to discuss with Brody. I heard Lance mumble something under his breath. "What did you say?" I asked.

Lance stopped walking for a moment, and stumbled over his words. "Oh, nothing much, actually. I was just kind of wondering if ... well, you see, there's a cattle auction in town on Friday afternoon. I'll be going, for work. With the number of animals we've lost recently, Clint and Jess decided we should concentrate on increasing our herd now so we don't have to change our menus later. I'm wondering if you might be interested in seeing it. I mean, that is, if you've never been to one before. And if you'd like to go. You never know, you may learn something that would help with your case."

That was an interesting thought. And it certainly couldn't hurt my investigation. I smiled at Lance. "That sounds really nice. I'd love to go." *Why not? It isn't like it would be a date or anything. Just additional research for my case.*

A wave of relief washed over Lance's face. "Great. I'll stop by your room around 1:00, if that's all right with you."

"I'll look forward to it," I told him. And I meant it.

We arrived at a fork in the road. "Here's where I get off," Lance said, pointing to the dirt road on the right. I'm guessing you know the way to the office from here."

I nodded. "I do."

"Okay. So I'll see you Friday then." He began to walk away, then stopped abruptly. "On, one more thing, before I forget. Would you mind giving this to Brody?" Lance reached into his vest pocket and pulled out what looked to me like a credit card. "He left it on the bar at the High Country Saloon the other night. I grabbed it when I realized it was his."

"No problem." I took the card from Lance. No question about whose card it was. Brody's name was on it. I was about to go on my way when a little bell went off in my head. "So you saw Brody at a bar recently?" I asked.

"That's right. I went there for dinner. And a beer or two. To make the most of my day off. I imagine you've heard that alcohol isn't allowed on the ranch?"

I nodded.

Lance continued, "I didn't sit with Brody, or anything like that. Just saw him there at the bar."

"What night was that?" was my next question.

Lance furrowed his brow. "Guess I'd have to say it was Sunday."

Sunday? Hmmm. "Around what time?" I asked.

"Couldn't have been much later than 6:30 or so. He walked by my table when he was fixing to leave. I invited him to sit a bit, and chat. Just to be friendly, though. I was pretty sure he wouldn't do it. And relieved when he didn't."

"And what did he do?"

"He said he couldn't join me. That he had to be some place. I figured he was talking about work. I'd heard him bitching in the afternoon about how he'd been put on the night shift again – the damn night shift, as he called it. Well, anyway, thanks for giving this back to him. I better get going. See you soon."

"Right." I stood there watching Lance's lovely buns walk away and wondering about Brody. The guy hadn't shown up for work on Sunday night. The night that Gus died alone in the hills. The question now became where was Brody that night? And why?

Chapter 16

The foreman, Jess Parker, was outside the ranch office speaking with a tall, lanky fellow that I assumed must be Brody. Jess had his hands on his hips and an angry look on his face as he glared up at the guy. Brody stood motionless looking down in Jess's general direction.

I heard Jess say, "Just do it."

Brody responded, "Whatever."

I couldn't see Brody's face, but my guess was that he was rolling his eyes. He was wearing what appeared to be new blue jeans and a neatly pressed white shirt beneath a fringed brown leather vest. His cowboy boots were shiny black with heels at least two inches high. They were also spotless. Overall, he was the perfect picture of a city slicker trying hard to look like a real cowboy.

I cleared my throat to alert them to my presence. "Good morning, Jess" I said. "It looks like it's going to be another lovely day. And you must be Brody. I appreciate you taking the time to answer a few questions for me." That was somewhat of a lie. I didn't simply appreciate his cooperation. I expected it. But it was usually best to start out playing nice.

Brody turned my way and removed his cowboy hat to reveal finely sculptured sideburns and a head of black hair slicked back off his forehead. "Morning, Ma'am," he said as he inclined his head toward me. "I'm more than happy to be of assistance." He hesitated, then gave Jess a nasty look. "The thing is, like I was just telling Jess here, this morning may not be the best time. We all need to be out rounding up the herd for today's head count."

Jess shook his head. "No need to worry about that, Brody. I'll pitch in with the rest of the guys. We'll get the job done in no time. I'll leave you in charge of things here. That way, you can speak with this lovely lady, take care of whatever else needs attention and still not get those shiny new boots dirty." He smirked ever-so-slightly and stared at Brody's boots.

"If you say so, Boss," Brody pouted, "But we'll still have to make it quick. Even without the head count, there's lots of work waiting to be done here this morning. We can't be wasting time with small talk." He flashed me a smile which appeared to stop at his lips.

"Take all the time you need," Jess said, his tone firm. "Some things are more important than others. Cattle rustling is one of those things." He frowned, then added, "Gus's death is another."

Brody smirked. "As you wish." He turned to me. "How about we sit ourselves down on the porch and have a nice little chat?" He strutted toward the building like a guy who thinks he's being charming but can't quite pull it off.

"By the way, Amy," Jess said, "you're more than welcome to hang around for the head count. That'd give you a chance to question the other cowboys if you've got a mind to do so. Besides, head counts always include a big lunch for the bunch of us. It adds a little fun to a tedious job. It's also one of the few times all the ranch workers are together. You might find it interesting."

"Thanks, Jess. That would be great."

Jess got in a dusty old black pickup and drove away. Brody dropped into a rocker on the porch, stretched his legs out, hands behind his head. "So, what can I tell you?"

I pulled a pen and notebook out of my purse and sat facing Brody on the porch. I decided to start with the easy stuff. "How long have you worked here?"

"Couple of years, I guess."

You guess? How can you not know? "Do you like it?"

"Like getting paid."

"How do you feel about herding cattle?" I asked.

Brody frowned. "It's OK. Like it better when the critters don't go missing, or showing up dead. The goings-on around here lately have been a bit of a downer."

"What about working the night shift? How do you feel about that?"

"Stupid waste of time and energy." Brody's voice raised as he said this. "Waste of good manpower, too. And it's not making a damn bit of difference. Cattle are still disappearing, or dying. There's got to be a better way to put a stop to that other than roaming around the hills in the middle of the night."

And as soon as you come up with one, please let us know. "I'm sure both Jess and Clint would love to hear any ideas you have." It was a struggle not to grin as I said this. Brody didn't seem to notice. I pushed on. "Why do you think a rustler would take only one animal at a time?"

"That's a tough one," he said. "Doesn't make much sense, does it? Any rustler worth his salt would be trying to take the whole damn herd at once."

At least Brody and I agreed on that point. "Have you given any thought to who may be doing this?"

A blank stare was his initial response.

I defaulted to my follow-up question. "Do you think anybody here at the ranch might be involved?"

He let his gaze wander around the ranch for a few moments. Finally he said, "Sure hope not."

Not helpful. "Let's talk about the night Gus died," I said. "It's my understanding that you were scheduled to work that shift with him."

Brody frowned. "Excuse me for saying so, but I thought you were here to look into cattle rustling problem."

"You're right. I am. Do you think that Gus's death may be somehow related?"

"Don't really see how it would be," he said. "Or why."

"Let's talk about it anyway. Just for the heck of it."

Brody shrugged. "Sure. Why not? It's your dime. I'm not sure what I can tell you, though. Don't forget. I wasn't there when he fell."

And therein may lie the problem. Perhaps Gus would still be alive if he hadn't been alone in the hills.

"So you're convinced it was an accident?"

That got Brody's attention. "Of course it was. What the hell else could it be?"

I decided not to respond to that. Let Brody wonder about it a bit. "What time did the night shift begin that day?"

"Same as usual. Ten o'clock. Shift runs until six in the morning. You know, the hours when an honest fellow ought to be sleeping."

"Did you usually work with Gus?" I asked.

Brody nodded. "At night, yeah. Day shifts, not so much."

"Were you two friends?"

"He and I got along just fine."

That was good to know, but it wasn't exactly what I had asked. "Did you work well together?"

"Well enough, I suppose."

"What did you normally do when you worked the night shift? Anything in particular?" I asked.

Brody snorted loudly. "We mostly just wasted our time looking for rustlers we were never going to find. Or dead cows. We got pretty good at finding them."

"What did you talk about?" I asked.

He gave me a funny look. "Not much. Other than where to look for stray cows. Or rustlers."

"Did Gus have any ideas about who the rustlers might be?"

"If he did, he didn't share that with me. Like I told you, we didn't waste time with idle chit chat. We were there to work, not for socializing."

"Yet you didn't work that night."

"Couldn't. I was ailing. Called in to let Jess know I couldn't make it."

I put down my notebook and looked Brody straight in the eyes. "As I understand it, you didn't actually speak with Jess. Is that correct?"

Brody shrugged. "It seems he wasn't available. I got the answering machine. Left a message telling him I was sick."

"So I heard. What exactly was the nature of your illness?"

"Stomach problems." He patted his belly as if to ensure that I understood. "Must have been something I ate."

"Something you ate at the High Country Saloon?"

Brody's eyes popped open wide. His mouth, however, remained shut.

"Lance told me he saw you there," I said.

"He could have been mistaken. You know, after a couple of drinks, all cowboys look pretty much alike." Brody grinned and studied his fingernails.

I couldn't help but notice that his nails were clean and well-manicured. Odd for a cowboy. I reached into my pocket and pulled out Brody's credit card. "Lance asked me to give this to you. Said you left it at the bar."

"Thanks. I've been wondering where that went," Brody said. "It was right nice of Lance to see that I got it back."

"What did you eat at the saloon that could have made you sick?" I asked.

"Steak and beans, same as usual."

"Was it good?"

"Good enough. Why?"

"So it didn't have a funny taste?" I asked, "Like maybe there was something off about it."

"Nope. Tasted just fine." He turned his head and checked the large clock on the porch wall. "I should start getting some work done now. Is there anything else you want to ask me?"

Actually, there was. "What if Gus's death weren't an accident? Do you have any thoughts on who might have wanted him out of the way? Or why?"

"Yes and no."

"What does that mean?"

He sighed, as if he were dealing with a backward child. "It means that if he had help falling into that ravine, I'm guessing it was probably the rustlers. Whoever they are. The why should be obvious."

"How so?"

"If they did it, they must have thought Gus was on to them. And they wanted to shut him up."

"Do you think he was on to them?"

Brody shrugged. "Beats me."

He put his hat back on his head and scowled at me. "And that truly is all I can tell you. Now, if you will excuse me, I have work to do." He rose and strode into the office as if he owned the place.

As the screen door slammed behind him, I stayed seated on the porch and reviewed the notes I had taken. I was sure I didn't care for Brody, but that was neither here nor there. I wasn't sure, though, if I had learned anything from him or not. Either he honestly didn't know anything about the problems on the ranch or Gus's death, or he knew a lot. Or maybe there was something else going on that I hadn't thought of yet. I'd let it bounce around in my head for a while before passing any judgment.

Chapter 17

I hung out on the office porch for the best part of an hour checking my email and adding to my notes. And letting my mind wander a bit as my eyes wandered around the property. Sometimes the best ideas came to me when I let my mind wander. I knew I was killing time, but that didn't seem to matter. I was curious to see what Brody might do with his time alone. So far, he stayed holed up in the office. Doing what?

I was about to call Peggy at the office when Brody joined me on the porch. "Just heard from Jess," he said, holding up his phone to be sure I knew how he had heard. "Says things are moving right along. The cattle should begin arriving within an hour, maybe an hour and a half at most. Thought you might want to prepare yourself before they get here. Or maybe head on back to the inn. Things will be getting noisy and chaotic."

"Thanks for the heads up."

He stared at my sandaled feet for a moment, then added, "Pickins tells me you two are planning to ride the range this afternoon. You might want to reconsider your choice of footwear. Sneakers or boots work better in a stirrup, particularly if you're not an experienced rider."

He had a good point, which annoyed me no end. I looked him up and down. "You're probably right. I wouldn't want anybody mistaking me for a city slicker." If Jess's ETA was on target, I had plenty of time to return to my room, change my footwear and still be back here in time for the cattle count. I stood and headed down the road.

I basked in the sunshine and cool breeze as I walked back to my room. The weather was once again pure delight. As I approached the building where my room was located, I saw a figure standing outside my door. It took a minute to place where I had seen him. Then it hit me. Steve What's-his-name from the front desk. What in the world was he doing here?

"Can I help you with something?" I called out to him.

He spun around like a top at the sound of my voice. "Oh, yes, hello there Ms. Lynch. I was just looking for you." He raised his hand to shield his eyes from the sun and squinted in my direction. His cheeks glowed a lovely shade of pink. Was it sunburn? Embarrassment? Rosacea? Hard to tell.

"Oh? What's up?" I sped up my pace until I was right in the man's face. "Has something happened?"

"No, no, not at all. Everything is just fine. But I thought you might want to know. The coroner has released Gus's body."

So soon? "That was fast."

Steve shrugged. "I guess. Not too much to do, though, when it's an accidental death. Anyway, the funeral service is tomorrow morning. I realize you didn't know him, but I thought you still might like to pay your respects. Pretty much everybody from Madonna, both the inn and the ranch, will be there. This place can get by with a skeleton staff for a couple of hours. I thought this could be a good opportunity for you to connect with a lot of folks at once. Might help with your investigation, you know what I mean?" He dangled an envelope with my name on it just beyond my reach.

I did know what he meant. And I agreed with him. What I didn't know was why he felt he needed to deliver this news in person.

It struck me as over-the-top service-wise. "Aren't you nice to think of me? You know, a text or a voice mail would have been just fine. I feel badly you felt you had to come all the way up here in person."

The blank look on his face suggested that he didn't hear the hint of sarcasm in my voice. "Not a problem," he said. "That's our way here at the Madonna Inn. We aim to please our guests. Service with a smile and all that."

He handed me the envelope. "Anyway, I guess I better be going now. Got to get back to work. It isn't good to leave the office unattended for too long."

He hurried off before I could respond to that.

Back in my room, I glanced at the info on the funeral, then tossed the paper on the table I'd been using as a desk. I'd deal with that in the morning. I noticed that my laptop was open and the screen was lit up. "Damn!" I scolded myself. "You know better than to leave things like that." I closed the lid and promised myself not to be so careless in the future.

It occurred to me that my purse might be awkward while riding a horse. I stuffed my phone, my notebook and pen into my jeans pocket and tossed the purse onto a chair. After verifying that my door was securely locked, I headed back out. Didn't want to miss the cattle count.

A cacophony of bovine sounds reached my ears as I neared the ranch. It surprised me that a mere 150 cattle could create that much noise. Not exactly a joyful noise either. It sounded more like groans of protest. Or perhaps a group of cows with stomach aches. Their hooves thundered on the ground as they drew nearer.

I crested the hill which overlooked the ranch office to see a large cloud of dust in the air and what, to my unschooled eyes, appeared to be a stampede. The cowboys hooted and hollered as they not-so-gently directed the cattle into a large corral. It amazed me that, despite their mournful groans, the cattle responded to the ranch hands' prodding. They made their way into the corral, nudging each other as if pushing their way into a bovine rock concert.

When the last of the animals entered the corral, Jess closed the gate and rode over to greet me. "I'm so glad you decided to join us," he said. "The trickiest part of our job is done now. Before we commence with the actual counting, we're taking a break for lunch, compliments of the Madonna kitchen staff. He pointed off to his left where a man in a chef's hat and apron stood working at a charcoal grill and placing platters of food on a long table.

"It's nothing fancy," Jess continued. "Just burgers and hot dogs. But you're welcome to join us."

"That'd be great. Thanks." I made my way to the grills where the cowboys had already dismounted and were filling their plates.

I helped myself to a burger and some potato salad, then looked around for someplace to sit and eat. I settled myself on a bench near a group of ranch hands. I recognized Lance and Pickins. Lance gave me a nice smile. Pickens nodded in my direction. The other ranch hands – one young, one old – were new to me. They were laughing hilariously as they looked at something on a cell phone one of them was holding.

"I can't believe you actually took a picture of that," one fellow guffawed. "But I'm kind of glad you did."

"Where did you take this?" Pickins asked.

"In the barn."

"When?"

"Sunday night."

Lance chimed in, "And they didn't see you coming? Or hear you?"

"Sure doesn't look that way, does it?" the older unknown guy laughed.

The fellow holding the cell phone said, "That's for sure. And this isn't the first time I stumbled onto the two of them, just like this. Sometimes in the barn, or behind the tool shed. Sometimes out in the hills. The other night was the first time I actually managed to get a picture.

"Do you know who she is?" Pickins asked.

The cell phone owner shook his head. "Don't know her name. I've seen her over by the main building, though. Think she works in one of the shops there."

Lance frowned and shook his head. "You guys really shouldn't be showing that picture around. Nothing good will come of it. And if Brody catches wind of it, lord knows what he might do. Never mind about the boss. No sense risking your job." Lance rose and strolled away from the group.

That did it. I had to know what was in that picture. And who. The question was how.

Chapter 18

Once lunch was over, the cattle count began in earnest. Jess stood just outside the gate with a clipboard and a tally counter. He monitored the operation while the cowboys checked each animal for any obvious problems then released it from the corral. He also clicked his tally counter to record the actual numbers as cows and bulls and steers passed by him one by one. Once outside the gate, the animals were directed back toward the hills in a cloud of dust by two cowboys on horseback.

The entire process took less time than I had imagined it would. Within an hour or so, the corral was empty, the recently freed cattle were nearly out of sight and the cowboys were riding off behind them to do whatever it was that cowboys actually did in the hills.

Only Jess and Pickins remained at the ranch.

Jess frowned as he finished adding up the numbers. "Son of a bitch," he exclaimed. "Not again."

Pickins and I watched him anxiously. My guess was that the count was off.

"Two more missing," Jess said at last. He looked up at me from his clipboard. "When we spoke the other day, I told you that we didn't usually get upset over finding one or two head missing. That they'd show up somewhere or other, so it really wasn't any big deal."

"Right," I said, remembering my conversation with Clint.

"That's not true anymore. We're down to 116 head. Having two cows gone missing has now become a major problem. Gotta get this rustling stopped before the entire herd is gone."

Neither Pickins nor I responded to his words. There was nothing we could say that would help. Jess walked toward the office shaking his head.

"Damn shame," Pickins said. "We've got to put an end to this now. How about you and I saddle up and ride the range? Maybe we'll find the two missing critters."

"That would be great," I told him. "I do want to check out the grazing areas as well and see where dead animals have been found. I'm not sure it will do any good, but it should give me a better feel for how things work. Maybe between the two of us we can figure out what's been going on, and come up with a way to put a stop to it."

"Amen to that," Pickins said. He led me to a small corral where two horses seemed to be awaiting our arrival. They were saddled up and raring to go.

Pickins broke into a big silly grin. "I guess this would be a good time to ask if you've ever ridden before."

"I have. But not in a long time. I hope that's not a problem."

"Not at all," he said. "It'll come right back to you, just like riding a bike. At least half of the inn guests who sign up to ride the trails have never been on a horse before. I've been dealing with that for years. Riding out with you ought to be a piece of cake."

I mounted my horse without assistance, did a couple of turns around the corral, and declared to Pickins that I was ready to roll. We rode out away from the ranch.

"So what did you think of the cattle count?" Pickins asked me.

"It was pretty interesting. And lunch was a nice treat. It was good to get a chance to see all of the ranch hands, even if I didn't get to speak with all of them yet."

"They're usually a pretty good group of guys. Sorry you had to see them misbehaving today."

I smiled, pleased that he brought it up. That saved me from appearing overly nosy. "What was that all about? Some kind of photo?"

Pickins snorted. "Yeah. Right. The wrong kind, I'm afraid."

I rode along beside Pickins trying to appear nonchalant. "Everybody certainly seemed to find it amusing."

"And they all ought to be ashamed of themselves. Rusty is old enough to know better. He's been here long enough to know that something like that is nothing but trouble. It would've been easier to excuse a young guy like Frank. But not Rusty."

"What was the photo of?" No sense beating around the bush.

"More like who," he answered.

I remained quiet, hoping he'd volunteer the information. He didn't. "And who was it?" I asked.

Pickins sighed mightily. "It was a picture of Brody. You know which one he is?"

"I do. We met this morning."

"And he wasn't alone. That girl was there with him. The one from the gift shop. Looks a lot like her sister in the restaurant."

"Do you mean Alexa?" I suggested.

"That's right. That girl never was any good. And I ought to know. I lived next door to her and her family for years. The whole lot of them were bad news."

"Are you sure that was her in the photo?" I asked.

"Sure am. And they were both buck naked and misbehaving something fierce. You might not want to hear the details."

He may have been right about that. Or not. You never knew how a little bad behavior and perhaps a bit of blackmail could affect an investigation.

Pickins continued, "From what I hear, this wasn't the first time either. Word is those two have been sneaking off in the night for a while now."

"Do you know what night that photo was taken?" I asked.

He shook his head. "Not for sure. A couple of nights ago maybe."

Could it have been Sunday? Might that be why Brody didn't show up to work with Gus? That was worth checking out.

Suddenly Pickins stopped dead in his tracks, his forehead full of worry lines.

"Is something wrong?" I asked.

"Maybe so." He pointed up ahead of us where several large birds were circling in the sky. "Vultures," he said. "Pall bearers in the sky. Something there has sure got their attention. Come on." He spurred his horse into a faster gait and rode toward the birds.

I followed.

The vultures scattered as Pickins arrived on the scene. He dismounted to get a look at whatever was attracting them. "You might not want to come any closer," he said to me. "What we have here is not a pretty sight."

"Just what do we have here?" I asked, approaching slowly.

"The sorry remains of whatever the coyotes feasted on last night."

I slid down off my horse and approached what appeared to be a shallow grave disturbed by the afore-mentioned coyotes. All that remained in the grave was a few pieces of torn clothing lying on top of a rotting lump of flesh and bones. My stomach lurched as my eyes surveyed the ground. I fought the urge to gag.

Something off to the left, and a few feet away, caught my eye. "Wait, Pickins. Come look at this."

"God no!" he cried as he moved closer. "Is that what I think it is?"

"It looks to me like a human hand," I said.

He bent down for a closer look. "You've got that right. And I'm sorry to say I know whose hand it is."

I waited silently.

"It's Don Huddleston's," he announced.

"How do you know?"

"See the ring on that finger? I'd know it anywhere. Don never took it off." He pointed to a thick silver band holding several tiny dots of turquoise.

"Holy shit," was all that I could say.

Pickins grabbed his phone and made a quick call. "The authorities are on their way," he told me. "They want us to wait here."

No surprise there. I sighed and leaned against my horse, stroking his mane. That was when I noticed a second hole in the ground, considerably smaller than the grave. It appeared to be recently shoveled out. It was empty.

"What do you think that is all about?" I asked.

Pickins shrugged. "Beats me."

I surveyed the terrain around us.

"Will they be able to get the sheriff's car out here?" I asked Pickins. "Or an ambulance? These roads look barely passable."

"Not a problem," he said. "Their vehicles are well-equipped to deal with these hills. Have to be, if they want to do their job." He hesitated a moment, then asked, "They're sure to have questions for us. Are you going to be all right with answering them?"

"I'll be fine." I pulled out my phone and began taking photos from every angle. Might as well document the area while waiting. Once the authorities arrived, they would declare it all a crime scene, which would limit access to the entire area. Before that happened, I wanted to gather as much detailed information as possible. I even photographed the empty hole.

When I finished, I turned to face Pickins. His sunburned face and sad eyes were a less disturbing sight than Don's hand. "Did you know Don well?"

He let out a long, sad sight. "Yup. I probably knew him better than most folks around here. For whatever reason, the guy decided to befriend me. I guess he needed someone to talk to. To confide in. He chose me."

Confide? Now that was an interesting verb. "What was going on with him? I heard he was a writer, but other people seemed to know about that."

"They did. He claimed to be doing research for a book about the local history here. That was no secret. But there was something else going on with him as well."

"What was it?"

"I don't rightly know," Pickins said. "But whatever it was, he said it would change his life for the better. Sometime soon. And that from then on, he said he'd be riding high."

Interesting. That sounded a lot like what Rosa's sister Alexa had told me. That things were about to change for them as well. It made me wonder if anybody else around here was expecting better days as well. And if so, who? And why?

Before Pickins had a chance to say anything more, two vans arrived with sirens blaring and lights flashing. One was marked Sheriff, SLO County, one the other SLO County Crime Scene Unit.

I looked down at Don's remains and frowned. Two ranch hands dead in a week. This was not good. It would be interesting to see what happened next. And to whom.

Chapter 19

I watched in a combination of fascination and abject horror as the crime scene techs meticulously studied, documented, photographed and bagged Don's remains. It was a nasty business, which they conducted with the utmost respect. That was nice to see. One of them, a petite young woman with dark curls peeking out from under her cap, looked up at me. "You can be grateful we're out here in the hills. If this mess were inside, the odor would be unbearable."

I took her at her word.

Pickins and I stayed at the scene observing the goings-on until the sheriff was ready to take our statements. The process was quick and painful. Eventually they ran out of questions and told us we could leave. We mounted our horses and rode silently back to the ranch.

Jess and Clint greeted us there. We exchanged a few sad words, then Clint handed me a pint of very nice single malt scotch. "Take this back to your room and try to relax," he said. "You've had a difficult day. We'll talk later."

I did as instructed. My cell rang around the time I was starting to relax. Peggy. Calling from the office.

"Don't you ever leave on time when I'm away?" I asked.

"Nope. I wait until both George and Mark have left, so they can notice how hard I work when nobody is watching."

I laughed. "So what's up?"

"You first," she said. "Your day was probably a lot more interesting than mine."

I struggled to relate the events of the day to her without reliving the emotions. The scotch helped. At least a little.

"Oh my God," she said when I finished. "That's beyond awful. What can I do to cheer you up?"

"You could begin by telling me the reason for your call," I suggested.

"Oh yeah. Right. I called you."

"Because...?"

"Because I have the information you wanted on the ranch hands."

"That was fast."

"What can I say? Without my boss looking over my shoulder, I was able to get it done quickly and still handle the rest of my regular workload."

"You are a marvel. Now tell me what you learned."

"OK. Here goes. I'll start with your new friend Lance Guerrero. 38 years old. Moved to San Luis Obispo as a child. Grew up there. High school graduate. No other formal education. No arrests. No police record. Clean driving history. Worked on a few other ranches in the general area. A couple of years at each. Ended up at the Madonna Ranch four years ago. Oh, and by the way, he is single."

"Good to know. Next?"

"Gale Pickins. Same story as Lance, just older. He's 64, to be exact. Always lived in San Luis Obispo. He has worked for the Madonna family for over forty years."

"Slow down a little here," I told her. "You know I don't take shorthand."

"Right. Sorry. Next comes Clint Jennings. Not only is he clean as a whistle, he's also a Madonna."

"How so?"

"He's married to Alex Madonna's daughter."

"Something he didn't mention. I wonder why."

"Don't wonder too long," Peggy said. "He has been there forever and both the inn and the ranch have thrived under him. From what I could find, it's the only job he has ever had. The same is pretty much true for Jess Parker. He's almost an institution at the ranch."

While I appreciated Peggy's thoroughness, so far none of that information was helpful. "Are they all that dull and squeaky clean?" I asked. *Please say no.*

"Rusty Daniels is. His story sounds like a replay of Pickins, except that he was born in San Mateo. After him, things get somewhat more interesting."

That was a relief. "How so?" I asked as I jotted down a few notes.

"Brody Knight is originally from Chicago. He moved to Hollywood in his teens with high hopes of becoming a star. It didn't happen. He moved on. But the photos I found of him sure look like he is still overly pleased with himself."

"Is that a stage name?" I asked.

"Must be. He was born Philip Harrison McGregor. Nothing too interesting in Phil's background either. Moving right along, there's Gus Delgado, may he rest in peace. He's originally from Texas, Austin to be exact. Worked for several years as an assistant PI at a detective agency. He gave that up a few years ago and landed at the Madonna Ranch. Interesting career move, don't you think?"

"That's for sure. So that just leaves the newly-deceased Don Huddleston and a fellow I haven't met named Frank Jones. Right?"

"Frank Jones was easy, but not in a good way. The man has no history whatsoever. Whoever he is, I guessing he used to be somebody else. And whoever that was, he probably had something to hide."

"Interesting. Also somewhat disturbing. I'll ask around here and see what I'm able to learn. What about Don Huddleston?"

"Right. I saved the best for last. He worked at three other ranches in the San Luis Obispo area before landing at the Madonna Ranch. He has been there a few years now. He's originally from Philadelphia. Has a BA in history from Pennsylvania State University. Minored in creative writing. And he is actually what, he claims to be."

"Explain, please."

"He is indeed a writer. Has two published works of non-fiction. Both dealing with what he calls his life-long hobby. From what I've seen, it looks more like an obsession."

"Spill it, Peg. What does he do?"

"He's a treasure hunter."

Chapter 20

Peggy's report on the Madonna personnel kept me up half the night. A lot of it was good mostly for eliminating folks from the list of possible rustling suspects. The information on Clint, Jess, Pickins, Rusty and Lance was pretty much what I expected. Brody's story wasn't any big surprise either. I could picture him as a somewhat sad Hollywood wannabe. I wasn't going to dismiss any of these guys arbitrarily, but I wasn't going to waste much time on them either.

Frank's lack of history disturbed me no end. Who was this guy? What was he hiding? Why was he here? And where would I even begin to research these questions? Peggy was a pro. If she didn't find anything on the man, I probably couldn't either. Not a good thing.

Even more disturbing was the information on both Don and Gus. What in the world would compel a private detective to move from Texas to California to work on a cattle ranch? Was Gus looking for a new career path? Or was he here on a detecting mission? Was Don expecting to find a treasure somewhere nearby? And why were they both now dead?

AVENGING MADONNA

Most of all, what did any of this information have to do with my rustling investigation? That was my primary focus. It was my job. My gut told me there was a connection. My gut seldom lied.

Too many questions. Too few answers. Too little sleep.

Time to go to Gus's funeral.

Both Pickins and Lance offered me a ride. I declined. Better to have my own vehicle handy in case something interesting came up. I threw on my good-for-every-occasion black dress and headed out.

The service was held in the newer part of an old cemetery. It was a short drive from the Inn. I was one of the first to arrive. A good plan, as this afforded me more opportunity to observe the other mourners. There was bound to be something of interest going on with someone.

A few dozen folding chairs were arranged in a semi-circle around the grave-site. An ancient looking catholic priest was there, properly attired for the occasion. He stood silently and watched as a hearse arrived and the undertaker's crew delivered a simple dark wood coffin.

Several vehicles all pulled up at once. I took a seat in the back row and watched as a variety of cars and pickup trucks discharged their passengers. Clint was accompanied by a woman I assumed to be his wife. She was pretty - tall and slender with dark hair laced with flecks of gray. An older woman was with them as well. She was dressed in a dark blue dress and pale blue shawl. Although she used a cane, she still managed to carry herself regally. Mrs. Madonna perhaps? Jess, Pickins and Rusty emerged from a shiny new black truck. Brody, Lance and a fellow I assumed to be Frank followed, their pickup a bit older and dirtier. That looked to be everybody I knew from the ranch.

Alexa from the gift shop arrived with Steve Damon from the front desk. The waitress who had been crying over Gus was alone, her eyes still red, her shoulders slumped. The older fellow who guarded the entrance to the famous men's room arrived, possibly leaving his post unprotected. Oh dear!

An official sheriff's vehicle pulled up. Walt Benson, the agent in charge of all things rustling got out, accompanied by a good-looking forty-something guy in khaki pants and a navy blazer. I watched as the two of them scanned the area for a moment. Then they headed my way.

Benson seated himself beside me. "Morning, Ms. Lynch. Nice to see you again, despite the unfortunate circumstances. How is your investigation going?"

"Well enough," I said. "Making progress." I was pretty sure that was the truth, although where the progress was leading remained a mystery.

"This here is Mike Griswold," Benson continued, displaying his missing tooth in the process. "He's the coroner for San Luis Obispo County. Mike, this is Amy Lynch. She's investigating the Madonna's rustling loss for the insurance company."

"Hello." I gave him what I hoped was my very best smile. After all, it certainly couldn't hurt to know the coroner.

"Nice to meet you," Griswold said. "So sad about Gus. We're all sure going to miss the guy."

"So you're a friend of Gus's?" I asked. *I was hoping you were here on official business and could help me crack my case.*

Griswold nodded. "Yup. He was one of the regular gang from the High Country Saloon. Gus won our annual pool tournament two years in a row. Beat me out both times. I couldn't resent it though. He was one hell of a good pool player, not to mention an overall nice guy."

"And here are the rest of the boys from the saloon," Benson said. "Darn nice of them to come."

I followed his gaze to the far side of the seating area. Five fellows in their mid-thirties, all wearing boots and cowboy hats, nodded in our direction.

Noticeably absent was Rosa from the restaurant. Apparently somebody had to remain behind and mind the store.

AVENGING MADONNA

The priest's remarks were brief and soulful. Either he had actually known Gus or he was a gifted speaker. Whichever it was, his words came across as sincere. He then asked if anyone wished to say a few words.

Clint rose to the occasion. Removing his hat, he said, "To the best of our knowledge, Gus had no close relatives. Mrs. Madonna has asked me to speak on behalf of everybody at Madonna Enterprises. We are all saddened by Gus's untimely death. He was everybody's friend, an excellent worker and an all-around good guy. He got along with all of us at the ranch, never caused any trouble. It is tragic that he left us at such a young age. He will be missed." Clint lowered his eyes for a few moments, put his hat back on his head and sat.

The priest scanned the crowd. "Anybody else?"

No takers.

The good father nodded solemnly. "Thank you all for coming. Let us pray for the soul of Gus Delgado. May he rest in eternal peace."

A heartfelt "Amen" rose from the crowd. The undertaker crew then did their bit, quickly lowering the casket into the ground. People began to mill around, as if nobody wanted to be the first to leave.

"Good morning, Amy," Clint said as he approached me. "Mrs. Madonna here wanted to say hello." He nodded toward the older woman. "This is Amy Lynch."

"How do you do?" she said. "It was so very kind of you to come this morning, particularly considering that you never met Gus."

"It seemed like the thing to do," I replied. "You folks at the inn and the ranch have all been so kind to me. You appear to be a very close-knit group."

"We are indeed," she said. "And it saddens me to think that it may all be coming to an end."

Clint gave her a surprised look.

"Please don't tell me it's because of the rustling," I said. "My company fully intends to make good on your claim."

"Of course you do, and I thank you for it. But I am beginning to wonder if it may simply be too late. I don't know how much longer I can handle the pressure."

"Pressure?" I asked. "Pressure from the rustling?"

"No. Pressure to sell. All of it. Both the inn and the ranch. Things haven't been going so well for a while now. Our finances are in trouble despite Clint's best efforts. And this rustling problem is making it so much worse. Selling would break my heart. But there may be no choice."

"Don't say that, Phyllis. Please," Clint said. "We'll work it out somehow."

I lapsed into full investigator mode. "Has somebody been pushing you to sell?"

She nodded. "We've had two offers. Both through lawyers. We don't know who the would-be buyers actually are. The lawyers are pushy, and not a bit subtle. I just want them to go away."

The pained look in her eyes nearly broke my heart. "I'll see what I can do to help with that. If we can put a stop to the rustling, maybe other things will change as well."

She gave me a tight, sad smile. "One can only hope. I wish you luck with your case. Nice meeting you."

Clint took her arm and escorted her to the car.

Pretty much all of the mourners beginning to depart. I scanned the thinning crowd and noticed Agent Benson and the coroner, Mike Griswold, heading out. I wanted to find a way to pick the coroner's brain. The good news was that their vehicle was just in front of mine. I hurried to my rental, attempting to appear casual.

Griswold smiled as I approached and looked me up and down with a little twinkle in his eye.

Hmm. This might just be my big chance.

"It was so nice to meet you," he said. "Maybe we'll run into each other again while you're here."

Music to my ears. "How about later today? Perhaps I could come to your office after lunch. I would love to get your professional opinion on a few things concerning my investigation." *Mostly things that are none of my official business, but what the hell?*

Griswold pursed his lips. "I'd be happy to help in any way that I can. But today won't work. But how about tomorrow? I've got some time available in the afternoon."

"That would be great." I grabbed a business card from my purse and handed it to him.

"One o'clock work for you?" he asked.

"Absolutely. See you then." Something hit me as I got into my car. I had not heard anybody at Gus's funeral mention Don's untimely death. Had they not learned of it yet? Were they more concerned today at saying good-bye to Gus? Or were they all too much in shock to deal with it a second death in a week? Figuring that out could be my next challenge.

Chapter 21

My chance encounter with the coroner was a good thing. It could only help to move my investigation along in what I felt was the right direction. I was convinced that the rustling, Gus's death and probably Don's death as well were somehow connected. All I needed to do now was prove it.

I wished I didn't need to wait another day to question the coroner. I also wished I could get a better handle on my investigation in general. I was beginning to feel like I was treading water and struggling not to drown. Most of all, I wished I could stop the rustling, arrest the rustlers and figure out how and why Gus and Don both died.

If only wishing for something could make it so.

I sighed and headed toward my rental car. And then it hit me – like a ton of bricks. Something my mother had told me more than once. When you enter a church – any church, anywhere – for the first time, you get three wishes. Hell, it was worth a try. And I knew the church I needed to visit.

My phone provided me with directions. I drove the short distance to the old San Luis Obispo Mission Church.

What a lovely sight it was, a charming old building surrounded by gardens that were peaceful and welcoming. The church had thick whitewashed adobe walls and a red tile roof. According to the notation on the façade, it was built in 1772. The interior was cool and restful, the walls adorned with a variety of religious paintings. Nice.

I seated myself in a pew in the rear and got busy with my wishes: #1, a successful conclusion to my investigation, including a halt to the rustling; #2, an answer to how and why both Gus and Don met their deaths; #3 a resolution to my relationship with Pete, one way or another.

That mission accomplished, I left the church and began to stroll around the mission gardens.

"Good morning," a voice from behind me said. "Didn't I see you earlier at the Delgado burial?"

I turned to see the priest who had officiated at the cemetery. Up close, he looked even older that he had at the grave site. Perhaps a little wiser too. His eyes were bright and alert, as if he never missed a thing.

"Yes, I was there. It was a lovely service. But so sad." I extended my hand to shake his. "I'm Amy Lynch."

"Were you a friend of the deceased?" he asked.

"Not exactly. But I knew pretty much everybody who was there. I felt I should be there."

The priest nodded, but didn't pursue that topic. "And I am Father Felipe, resident pastor of the mission church."

"What a wonderful place to work," I said. "So peaceful and relaxing."

That brought a sad smile to Father Felipe's face. "Interesting choice of words. The truth is that neither this mission, nor San Luis Obispo County in general, has ever been known for being peaceful. Not for hundreds of years."

"Why is that?" I asked, intrigued by his statement.

His eyes brightened. "So you are not familiar with the history in this part of California?" He appeared eager to enlighten me on the subject.

I shook my head. "No, but I would love to hear about it."

"And I would love to tell it to you," he said. "Local history is a particular interest of mine. Always has been. Why don't you and I relax in the shade and we can have a nice long chat?"

He led me to a bench on the garden path. We sat. I listened.

"The Mission of San Luis Obispo is one of the oldest buildings in California" he began. "It was built in 1772, before there was even a town here. It supported the local Indian tribes as well as the ranchers. The land around here was well-suited for raising cattle. That made it quite valuable. It also made the ranchers rich."

I remembered my discussion with Clint about cattle ranching. "As I understand things, it wasn't just about selling the beef. The hides were important as well."

He smiled. "You understand correctly. The hides were a far more valuable commodity than the beef. Believe it or not, there was a time they were used as a medium of exchange. People referred to them as California bank notes."

"How long ago was that?" I asked.

"From the very beginning," he said, "During the Mexican period. Long before California became part of the United States, the local ranchers were quite prosperous."

I searched my memory banks, but failed to come up with the year when that had happened.

"That was back in 1850," he told me.

"Wasn't that around the time the gold rush began?" At least I remembered something from my high school history class.

"It was. And because of the gold rush, the ranchers became richer and richer, almost overnight."

"But didn't the gold rush take place further north?" I asked. I was pretty sure I had that fact right.

"It did. The actual digging for gold happened well north of here, up by Sacramento."

Now I was confused. "So how did the ranchers down here profit from it?"

AVENGING MADONNA

"The miners needed to eat," he replied. "And there were thousands of them. All of them hungry. The cattle raised around San Luis Obispo was crucial for their survival."

I conjured up a map of California in my mind. "That sounds like a very long road to travel for supplies."

A solemn look passed over the priest's face. "A long road indeed. And a dangerous one as well. You must bear in mind that the miners who were traveling south to purchase meat had their pockets full of gold. They provided an easy target for highwaymen."

I hadn't thought of that, but it made perfect sense.

"There was one particular highwayman who became quite well-known and eventually became the inspiration for the legend of Zorro."

"Oh? How so? Was he different from the others thieves?" *Perhaps he was more of a Robin Hood.*

"As the story goes" the priest said, "a group of gold miners who had come south brought with them a virus. This killed a number of local ranch workers as well as the young wife of the fellow in question. He vowed to avenge his wife's death and became a highwayman. He robbed the miners of their gold, murdered them and, as legend has it, cut off an ear from each victim as a souvenir."

"How dreadful," I said. "But the Zorro I remember was one of the good guys, not a murderer and a robber."

"Yes. The legend has changed considerably over time."

"Did they ever catch this man?"

"Eventually, yes. And vigilante justice prevailed in the end."

"Why vigilante justice?"

Father Felipe frowned. "That's all there was around here back then. San Luis Obispo County was the single most lawless place in America. There were times when it seemed as if everyone was fighting with everyone. Shoot-outs in the streets were common. Folks arguing over anything and nothing. And if shooting at a fellow didn't work, all a man had to do was accuse a person of wrong-doing, then get together a posse of like-minded people to hunt him down and punish him once and for all."

That didn't sound right to me. "Didn't they have lawmen? And judges and juries and jails?"

"They did. But pretty much all the lawmen, judges and juries were bought and paid for in advance. Any trials that they held were decided even before they began. As I said, vigilante justice.

The priest paused and looked around the mission courtyard. "After the trials, they'd bring the prisoners here to the Mission to be hanged. Just to ensure everybody got to see it. The convicted party was given the right of statement, to say whatever he cared to say in his own defense."

"Wasn't it a bit late for that?"

Father Felipe shrugged. "You'd think so, wouldn't you? Anyway, after that, the priest would administer the last rites to the prisoner. Then they'd hang him. Right over there." He pointed to a spot in the garden within full view of the street.

"Whatever happened to this fellow's gold?"

The priest gave me a wry smile. "Perhaps the highwayman's family used it to pay their property taxes. Or maybe the vigilantes seized the gold and split it amongst them. I like to think it somehow ended up in the hands of local widows and orphans."

That was a nice thought. Not highly likely though.

I had one more question. "When all this violence was happening, what were they all arguing about?" I asked. "It must have been something pretty important to result in shootings and hangings."

"It was mostly about the land. About who owned it. And who had stolen it from whom. There was a lot of feuding going on in those days. Some feuds lasted for generations. So much violence." He shook his head. "In the end, it's always about the land."

Chapter 22

The priest's lesson in local history left me feeling somewhat down. So much violence. That was always unsettling. I needed a diversion. I also needed to take a fresh look at my investigation. To re-examine what I knew so far and figure out where to go from there.

I knew exactly how to do all this. I called Pete. I'd been avoiding him long enough. And a fresh point of view could be exactly what I needed.

"Hello, Ames! I was just thinking about you. Planning on calling you as soon as I got home."

That made me smile. "Are you still at the office? Did I catch you at a bad time?"

"Not at all," he said. "I'm just finishing up for the day. Moira's got a few things left to do, then she'll close the office. I've got to tell you, that girl is a marvel. Hiring her was one of my better moves."

"I'm glad she's working out so well," I said. "Does this mean you have some time to talk? Or at least listen. I am in serious need of a well-trained analytical brain. May I bounce a few things off you?"

"Bounce away."

I spent the next half hour or so updating Pete on the current state of my investigation, life and death at the Madonna Inn and what

I knew, or didn't know, about anything and everything so far. He was a good listener.

"So what do you think?" I asked. "Am I missing something that should be obvious to me? I believe I'm on the right track, but now I need to figure out where to go from here."

"Is that all?" he said with a laugh.

"For now, yes."

There were a few moments of near silence as I listened to the wheels spinning in his head. Finally he said, "I've got two thoughts."

"That might just be two more than I have. Let's hear them."

"First of all, why did the coroner release Gus's body so quickly? Was he that sure it was an accidental death?"

"Good point," I said. "And what else?"

"We know that Don was murdered. Do we have any idea why? As you often say, there is no such thing as coincidence. That's the route I'd suggest."

"And a good route it is," I said, nodding my head as if he could see it.

We chatted a little while longer. It felt good to catch up on each other's life. He told me he loved me, and sounded like he meant it. I said the same, and hoped that it was so. Maybe my recent ambivalent feeling were just a fleeting thing. Maybe being up close and personal with two recent deaths had changed my perspective. I'd figure it out eventually.

I gave some thought to what Pete had suggested. My meeting with the coroner couldn't come soon enough. In the meantime, I could work on the questions concerning Don's death. And I had an idea of where to begin. I checked my watch. Still early afternoon. I grabbed my phone and called Jess at the ranch.

"Hello, Amy," he said. "Wasn't that a nice service this morning?"

"It certainly was."

"Seeing as you're calling me now, I'm guessing there might be something I can do for you."

I laughed. "You'd be correct. I have a favor to ask of you."

"Whatever you need," he said. "All you've got to do is ask."

"Do you still have the note Don Huddleston left saying he was leaving the ranch?"

"Sure do. Got it right here in my desk drawer. At first, I didn't quite know what to do with it. Got my answer now, though, since he's turned up dead. Gotta give it to the sheriff. He's coming by tomorrow morning to pick up Don' things. Maybe this note will help find the killer."

Tomorrow morning? Oh dear. That meant I needed to act fast.

"You're absolutely right," I told him. "Have you gone through Don's things to see if there's anything else of interest?"

"Nope. I was planning to do just that this afternoon."

That was good news. "I was hoping to take another look at the note. Just in case it's connected to my investigation. And I could help you sort through his things at the same time."

"That's right nice of you," Jess said. "I'd be glad for the help. If you have the time, that is."

"I have the time right now." I said, not even worrying about being pushy.

"Well then, come on down."

I changed out of my funeral clothes in a flash and headed out. It was amazing how quickly I could move when properly motivated. I made it to the ranch in no time.

Jess was waiting for me on the porch. "Howdy. Why not have a seat while you take a look at Don's note?" He handed me a manila envelope. "Got it right here."

I sat and opened the envelope. A piece of lined paper torn from a notebook was folded inside. A childish scrawl of black ink simply said: "I'm outa here. Quitting as of now. Hasta la vista." The letters were oversized, all in caps and occasionally not on the line.

"Don didn't write this," I said.

"How do you know?"

"The man was a writer. He had two books published and was apparently working on a third. Neither this handwriting nor the questionable spelling belongs to a published author."

Jess stroked his chin. "I see what you mean. And I know what that means. Don didn't write this because Don didn't quit. And whoever it was that did write this note must be the person who killed him."

Bingo! "So it would seem," I said. "And now we're faced with two questions. Who killed Don? And why?"

"Isn't it the sheriff's job to figure that out?"

"Of course. But it's mine as well. I can't help but wonder if Don's death is related to the rustling claim. I've always worked well with the authorities in the past. There's no law that says we can't help the sheriff out a bit now." I stood up. "How about we go take a look at the rest of Don's things?"

"You've got it."

Jess led me into the bunk house. There were six beds with a small trunk at the foot of each. The place was nothing fancy. – small and void of any decoration – but it was surprisingly clean. "This here was Don's bed," Jess told me, pointing to a bunk by the rear window. He hoisted the trunk nearby and deposited the contents onto the bed. "And here's his stuff."

We began to sort through the sorry little pile. Don had little in the way of clothes, just an extra pair of jeans, a couple of heavy cotton shirts, a few changes of underwear, three pairs of socks with holes in them and a winter jacket lined with sheepskin. Apparently the guy didn't dress up much. There were also a few basic toiletries. Nothing much of interest yet.

Then we examined his paperwork. Two spiral notebooks contained what appeared to be his research notes, all in handwriting far superior to that in his farewell letter. There was a well-worn paperback book on legends of the old west. No surprise there based on what Peggy had told me.

There were a few other books as well. The dust cover identified one of them as the History of the Flora and Fauna of the Southwest.

Jess snorted as he read the title. "Good grief, doesn't that look boring? You've got to wonder about a guy who'd want to sit around reading this stuff."

I wondered as well. I took the book from him to examine it more closely.

"And what about this?" Jess asked. "What the heck do you think he needed a Spanish-English dictionary for?"

"Probably for this," I said.

"Huh?"

"This isn't what it looks like, Jess. That cover was just a ruse. To disguise this." I held up the book in my hands. The title on the inside cover read Diario.

"The guy kept a diary?" Jess asked.

"Not Don," I said. "Look here." I pointed to the opening page. It contained a simple statement – Diario de Elena 1850 – in lovely cursive handwriting. "I'm thinking Don disguised this for a reason."

Jess's eyes grew wide.

I felt like we may have hit paydirt.

"Did you say that the sheriff is coming tomorrow to collect Don's things?" I asked.

Jess nodded. "That's right. Around nine o'clock, he said. Don't know why he didn't take these things when he was here the day Don's body was found. Guess he had bigger problems on his mind at the moment. When I saw him at the burial this morning, he said he had a busy afternoon ahead of him and that tomorrow would be better to come get this stuff."

That put a smile on my face. "Would it be all right with you if I took this diary back with me to look at this evening?"

"What the heck for? It's in Spanish."

"I studied Spanish in college," I told him. "Besides, I've got Don's dictionary to help me."

Jess looked doubtful. "I don't know. The sheriff might not look kindly on that."

"He doesn't have to know about it. I could look it over tonight then get it back to you first thing in the morning. Long before the sheriff arrives."

Jess's frown grew larger.

I favored him with my pitiful female look, a ruse I had practiced over time. It had worked well for me on many occasions.

"Oh, all right," Jess said. "I guess it couldn't hurt nothing. But it's got to be our little secret. If the sheriff finds out, there could be hell to pay."

I crossed my heart with my fingers. "Won't tell a soul. Promise."

Jess relented. I rejoiced.

I'd stay up all night if I had to. Something told me It would be worth my while.

Chapter 23

I was up before dawn Friday morning jam-packing my weary body with cup after cup of strong black coffee. I needed to coax myself into action after barely two hours sleep. And I needed to do it quickly. The sheriff was coming at 9:00 to pick up Don Huddleston's belongings from Jess. I wanted to return the diary and dictionary to Jess well before that time, just in case the sheriff showed up early.

My exhaustion didn't matter. It was worth the effort to read well into the wee hours of the morning. And the dictionary was a life-saver. Elena was a prolific writer. She chronicled the details of daily life on her California cattle ranch in lovely cursive handwriting. It was interesting enough, though hardly relevant to my case ... until shortly after 3:00 A.M.

Then ... bazinga! The final few pages were a combination of a lightning bolt and a gift from Heaven. My heart raced as I read...

> *"**Mi hijo esta muerto**. My son is dead. They hanged him today in the courtyard of the mission. It broke my heart even though I knew I couldn't plead his innocence as a defense. He was **a bandido**, a highwayman. He had robbed and slaughtered many men. There was no doubt of that.*

There was no use in arguing that his trial was unfair. For as long as I remembered, local justice had been nothing but a sham. Judges and juries were bribed. Outcomes were pre-determined. There was no true justice to be had in San Luis Obispo County. And my Diego was the victim of that corruption.

I alone know the reason behind his life of crime: his hell-bent commitment to avenge the death of his wife Juanita. In his troubled mind, the gold miners had killed his wife and they needed to pay. This may have been wrong, but it was heartfelt. I'm not seeking to excuse his crimes, but rather to explain them.

My only consolation is in the fact that I, and I alone, know where the gold he stole is buried. 'It's there if you need it, Mama,' he had told me. 'Out in the hills, by your grandfather's unmarked grave below the twisted sycamore tree. Only you would know where to find this gold. Use it well.'

I haven't used it yet, but I do take comfort in knowing that the gold is there. I'll know when the time is right. Only then will I make use of this, the final gift from my baby boy. Rest in peace, my son. **Descanse en paz.**

I wiped a tear from my eye, then thought *Hmmm. The same story the Mission priest had told me.* I couldn't help but wonder how this diary ended up among Don Huddleston's belongings. Or why.

After a few hours of fitful sleep, I dashed to the ranch office to return the diary to Jess. The place was empty. I walked over to the bunk house. No Jess there either. I left the diary with the rest of Don's things and headed back to my room, disappointed that I didn't have the chance to tell Jess what I had learned. It might have been helpful to watch his reaction, just in case he already knew about it. My heart told me he was one of the good guys, but my heart has been mistaken on occasion. At any rate, I expected that the sheriff would tell him all about it at some point.

I texted Peggy as soon as the office opened in Cambridge and asked her to set up a zoom with the two of us and Tiffany, the other member of our team. It was time to get a fresh perspective on this investigation. And Tiffany had a particular talent for doing exactly that.

We connected around mid-morning.

Peggy was her usual bright cheery self. "Good morning. How are you? Sam sends his love and says 'woof.' He's holding up bravely in your absence."

That was good to know. I liked having my canine friend nearby when I worked on a case. He was a wonderful listener. Often times, that was all I needed to get the job done.

"Thanks," I said. "Please give him a big hug for me. And perhaps a treat. Now, tell me: how are you ladies doing holding down the fort?"

"Fine. Things have been fairly quiet this week. Your case is the most interesting thing going on at the moment." Peggy paused and came up for air. "I've filled Tiffany in on everything we know so far."

"Hello, Tiff. I'm glad you could make it. We really need your input here," I said.

"Good morning, Amy." Tiffany waved and smiled at me. "We can't wait to hear the latest updates."

I was happy to oblige, giving them all the latest news. I ended with Elena's diary. "So, what do you ladies think? Including what appears to be obvious. That matters too, you know. Sometimes the answer is right in front of your face and you don't even see it."

"And just what is the obvious?" Tiffany asked.

Peggy decided to answer that. "Well, we know we're dealing with both cattle rustling and cowhands dying."

Tiffany raised her hands up into a "time out" position. "Stop right there, please. We need to clarify something."

"And what might that be?" I asked.

"Is it really rustling if they only take one cow at a time? I mean, why not just grab the whole darn herd at once and get it over with? And what about the cows they kill and leave out in the hills somewhere. What's that all about?"

"Good point, Tiff," I said. "I was wondering the same thing. So where does that lead us?"

"Maybe it isn't about the cattle at all," Peggy suggested. "Maybe that's merely a diversion, to cover up something else."

I gave that some thought. "I agree. Perhaps it's a form of harassment. Or a not-so-subtle threat."

"A threat of what?" Tiffany asked. "And from whom?"

"From parties currently unknown," I said, "but the threat is definitely there. It's suggesting to somebody at Madonna that bad things may continue to happen until he, or she, does what they want."

Peggy chimed in. "And what might these unknown parties want?"

"Apparently, they want to buy the place, both the inn and the ranch. All of it. I spoke with Mrs. Madonna yesterday. She told me there have been offers. She's not sure from whom. The potential buyers are working through an attorney. Mrs. Madonna made it very clear that she is definitely not interested in selling at this time."

"Interesting development," Peggy said. "Then what is the real issue here? Do you think somebody wants to run the inn and keep the cattle ranch going or to find the gold that may be buried there?"

Before I could voice my response, Tiffany broke in. "Do you believe there really is gold there?" she asked.

"I'm not 100% sure" I told her, "But between the dead or stolen cattle and the deceased cowhands, it appears that someone believes there is."

"OK. So who would know about this buried gold?" Peggy asked.

"Anybody who has read the diary," Tiffany said. "It could also be the subject of a local legend."

"And there's also Elena's descendants," I offered. "There could be some family lore that talks about it."

"And the way to find the gold is to figure out exactly who Elena was and where she lived," Tiffany said. "And if she is connected with the Madonna property."

"How do we do that?" Peggy asked.

A little bell went off in my head. "I believe I know how. And it should be easy."

"Easy?" Peggy said. "OK, let's hear it."

"The priest who told me the story of Diego the highwayman should know. He must have records of hangings and burials at the mission. I believe it's time for me to pay him another call."

"I have a question," Tiffany said. "It may not be important, but I can't help but wonder about something."

"About what?" I asked.

"How do you think Don Huddleston got Elena's diary? I mean, I know he was a treasure hunter, but still ..."

"That's a good question," I agreed. "Though we may never find the answer to that."

We sat in silence for a few moments to digest everything we had discussed. Finally Peggy spoke up. "You know, it may be exactly like the priest said."

"What do you mean?" Tiffany asked.

I answered that. "It may be simply all about the land."

Chapter 24

I headed into town as soon as our zoom meeting ended. There were a few things I wanted to check out.

My first stop was at the Mission. I found the priest sitting on a bench in the garden enjoying the morning air.

"Hello, Father Felipe. Do you remember me?"

He smiled up at me. "Indeed I do. From the burial the other day. And our nice conversation in the garden. How nice to see you again. Please, have a seat."

I sat.

He looked at me expectantly. "Is this a social call, or is there something I can do for you this morning?"

I liked a person who didn't beat around the bush. "I have a question," I said. "About something you told me yesterday."

He nodded and waited.

"The story you told me about the highwayman who was hanged here. Do you know his last name?"

"Martinez. Diego Martinez. He came from an old family. They had been here for generations. Does that name mean anything to you?"

I wasn't entirely sure how to answer that. "It may. In fact, it may be the clue to a good many things." Something else occurred to me. "Do you remember what year he was hanged?"

He furrowed his brow for a moment. "It had to be somewhere between 1855 and 1860. If it's important, I can check the records."

"That won't be necessary. Those dates are good enough. Thank you."

"My pleasure."

I stayed for a few minutes chatting with Father Felipe. He was a charming man, and quite knowledgeable about local history. I wished I could have remained longer, but duty called. Perhaps another time. Thanking him for his assistance, I headed out to my next destination: San Luis Obispo Town Hall. With the information I now had from Father Felipe, it would be interesting to trace the ownership of the Madonna land.

The clerk in the records department, an older woman with frizzy white hair and a beautiful smile, perked up as I entered the room. The nameplate on her desk identified her as Cecilia Perkins. "Good morning. Is there something I can help you with?"

"I need to check on some property records."

"You've come to the right place," she said. "What property are you interested in?"

"Madonna. Both the inn and the ranch." I handed her my card. "It's in connection to a case I'm investigating. I'm hoping to see the records going back as far as possible."

"Not a problem." She rose from her desk. "The older records are this way."

I followed her down a hallway and into a small, dusty room bursting with old wooden file cabinets.

She frowned as she looked around the room. "Please believe me that the current records are in much better order than this. The further back you go, the messier things become. And just to keep things interesting, the record-keeping systems have changed considerably over the years."

"It's my understanding," I said, "that the Madonna family purchased the land around 1950. I'm looking to learn who owned the land before them, and to trace ownership back as far as possible."

"I can help you with that," the clerk said. "Have a seat here and we can get started."

"That really isn't necessary," I protested. "I'm sure I can manage on my own. I don't need to take you away from your job."

"Not to worry. It's pretty quiet in here at the moment. I'm happy to help."

Less than thirty minutes later, I left the building with a smile on my face and a song in my heart. And the information I needed in my hands.

The history of the land turned out to be simpler than expected. Since record keeping began, the property had only three owners. The Madonna family bought it from a fellow named Henry Goff III, the great grandson of the original Henry Goff. He took possession of the land in 1860. The owner prior to that time, the only other owner on record, was listed as Guillermo Martinez. My guess was that he had a wife named Elena. And perhaps an outlaw son named Diego.

And perhaps a pot of gold buried somewhere on his property.

If the need arose, I could probably verify most of these facts by the records at the mission. Odds were the Martinez family attended masses there. The alleged gold, however, was another story.

It didn't take long for me to decide my next step. I sat on a bench outside City Hall and grabbed my phone.

"Hello. Madonna Inn. This is Steven speaking. How may I help you?"

"Steve, hello, this is Amy Lynch from New England Casualty and Indemnity. I'm hoping to speak with Clint if he's available.

"Hold on please and let me check."

I held. He checked. It didn't take long.

"Found him," Steve said. "I'll connect you now."

"Amy, hi. How're you doing? I was actually planning on calling you later today. Just to touch base on how your investigation is going. Yesterday at the funeral wasn't the right time or place for shop talk." He paused, but not long enough for me to get a word in. "Anyway," he continued, "I'm hoping you have some good news for me today. Between burying poor Gus and losing more cattle and finding Don dead, we're having one hell of a bad week."

"That's for sure. It has been rough. And I'm sorry to say I don't have any real news for you. At least not yet. But I could use your help with something."

"Whatever it is, I'll do what I can for you. Ask away."

"Mrs. Madonna mentioned yesterday that there have been two offers to buy the Madonna property."

"That's right."

"And they have both been made through lawyers. right?"

"Very aggressive lawyers," he said.

"Do you have any idea who the prospective buyers are?" I asked.

"Does it matter?"

"It might." That was all I dared tell him at the moment. No point in getting his hopes up that things would be better any time soon.

"Hmmm. Let me think about that."

I held my breath and listened to dead air while he thought.

It didn't take long. "I'm not real sure this will work," he began, "but I am acquainted with one of the lawyers in particular. Never really liked the guy, but that's neither here nor there."

That sounded encouraging. "And ...?"

"And I may be able to wheedle some information out of him if I play it right."

"What do you mean?"

Clint let out a long, low sigh. "It means perhaps I have something on the man. Something he may not want to go public. Now, mind you, it's not in my nature to go threatening folks, or anything like that. In this case, though, if I ask real nice, I'm thinking he may be willing to give me a name. Let me see what I can do."

Chapter 25

I arrived at the San Luis Obispo Coroner's office shortly after 12:30. My appointment with Mike Griswold was for 1:00. I sat on a bench in front of the building and reviewed my notes and questions concerning the deaths of both Gus and Don. A few minutes before 1:00, I entered the building to find Mike waiting inside. He had my card in his hand.

"Good afternoon, Miss. Lynch" he said. "Or is it Mrs?"

"It's Amy," I told him. "No need to be using fancy titles."

"Right. Sure. And you can call me Mike. I thought I'd wait for you here and save you the trouble of trying to track me down inside. Some folks don't enjoy passing through the work area of the morgue. I can take you the other way."

That was a relief. "Thanks"

I followed him into the building. It was a short walk to his office, a sterile, windowless room in need of a good dusting but otherwise reasonably neat and clean. I helped myself to the visitor's chair across from his desk. "I appreciate you taking the time to speak with me today."

He gave me a big, toothy smile. "It's my pleasure. It's nice to see you again. We didn't get much chance to chat at the burial yesterday. And I'd certainly like to get to know you better."

I favored him with a big smile, hoping to encourage his cooperation, then pulled out my phone. "Do you mind if I record this?"

"Not at all." He studied my card for a moment. "So you're an insurance investigator?"

"Yes. My company insures the Madonna Enterprises. I'm looking into recent events at the ranch."

"Like Gus's death?"

"Actually, the original focus of my investigation was the cattle rustling," I told him. "Since then, the two unexpected deaths there have complicated things quite a lot." I didn't mention to him that I was stepping outside my actual mission. That would have been counter-productive. "I'm assuming you've heard about the rustling problems."

"Sure. Everybody has. It's kind of a big deal for folks in the cattle business. It's been a while since that sort of thing has happened around here. And the part that makes no sense at all is those cows simply being killed and left in the hills. What do you suppose that's all about?" he asked.

"That's what I'm here to find out. And, hopefully, to help put a stop to it, and prevent similar problems in the future."

"I wish you luck with that. Then they wouldn't need to run a night shift. Gus sure hated working on that."

"Why so?"

"He was a people person. Being out in the hills like that, pretty much alone, didn't set well with him at all. Did what he had to do though. He needed the job." The coroner frowned, then changed the subject. "So, what did you want to ask me about?"

"Let's begin with Gus's death."

He made an open-palms gesture with his hands. "Ask away."

"From what you said at the burial, I'm guessing you and Gus were friends. It's always difficult to lose a friend, particularly someone so young. I'm sorry for your loss."

"Thanks." The coroner paused. "We're sure going to miss Gus at the High Country Saloon."

"And performing an autopsy on a friend must have been painful."

"That's for sure." The coroner sighed and stared out the window. "You said you wanted my professional opinion on something?"

"That's right." I glanced at my notes for a moment. "Gus's body was discovered on Monday morning. You released it for burial on Wednesday. Is it normal for things to move so quickly in this part of the country?"

"It was a bit faster than usual," he said. "Things had been pretty quiet around here the past few weeks. We were all caught up when Gus's body came in. And the cause of death was obvious. There seemed no reason to prolong things."

"What about his family?" I asked. "Were they not able to come to the burial?"

"According to Jess, there was nobody."

I found that sad. "I guess that makes sense," I said, then added, "Let's talk about the cause of death."

He shrugged. "Gus died due to trauma from a fall of twenty-odd feet. What's there to say?"

"We know he died when he landed at the bottom of the ravine," I said. "But I'm not entirely convinced that's the whole story."

"What do you mean? Am I missing something?" he asked.

"How did Gus get there?"

"He fell."

"Perhaps we need to look at how he came to fall. Did he trip? Lose his balance?" I paused quite deliberately, giving the coroner a moment to think. "Or was he pushed?"

"Shit!" Mike's eyes opened wide. "Please pardon the language. That thought sure took me by surprise. And I have to tell you, I'd have serious trouble believing that somebody pushed him. Why in the world would you think such a thing?"

"Because the troubles at the ranch didn't end there. There is also the issue of Don Huddleston's untimely death."

"Don Huddleston was shot. Took a bullet right to the head. What's that got to do with Gus?"

"Do you find it odd that both of these deaths occurred within a few days?"

The coroner furrowed his brow. "Are you suggesting that they might be somehow related?"

"I believe it's a definite possibility. Particularly with the issue of stolen or killed cattle. It can't all be merely coincidence."

He gave me a dubious frown. "I get what you're saying. I really do. But where does that leave us?"

"With a question or two about Gus's death. I'm wondering if perhaps a second look at things may be in order."

The coroner held his hands up in a gesture of surrender. "I'm not disagreeing with you. But what could we do now? It's too late. The body's already in the ground."

He sat back in his chair and stared at the ceiling. "You're not asking us to exhume Gus's body, are you? That's usually frowned upon. That is, unless there's a serious reason for it. And in this case, it'd be a waste of time. No matter how Gus got to the bottom of the ravine, he died as a result of his fall."

While I couldn't argue with that, I wasn't about to give up easily. "Is there any way you could look further into things?"

"Like how?"

After a moment of thought, I asked, "Was Gus buried in the clothing he was wearing when he died?"

Mike shook his head. "Nope. The funeral director told me Jess found some cleaner duds with Gus's belongings in the bunk house. They used those."

"Do you know what happened to the rest of his things?"

"You'd need to ask Jess about that."

"What about the clothes Gus was wearing when he fell? Where are they?"

"They're still here. In the evidence room. I was planning to throw them out this afternoon."

"Before you do that, would you mind taking another look at them?"

"Looking for what?" he asked.

"I don't know. Not yet anyway. But it's worth a shot, don't you think? Maybe you'll notice something that doesn't seem quite right." I did my best to give him my maiden in distress look.

It worked.

He sighed. "All right. You're a nice lady. For you, I'll take a stab at it. But I'm not making any promises here."

"Sometimes a stab is all it takes." I crossed my fingers, hoping that was so.

Chapter 26

I spent Saturday morning with my laptop, updating the computer files on the status of my investigation, such as it was. The exercise made me feel as if I was actually working. This mattered because I was planning to spend the afternoon at the cattle auction with Lance. I was pretty sure that would be an interesting experience. It would be a bonus if it included something which helped my case as well. Time would tell.

Unsure of the proper attire for a cattle auction, I opted for skinny jeans and a light blue cashmere sweater set. Not having brought boots, my sneakers would have to do.

Lance knocked on my door at precisely 11:30, all duded up in a leather vest and newly polished boots. Good look.

Once in his truck and on the road, Lance said, "Just so you know, my mission today is two-fold."

"How so? I assume you'll be looking to purchase some cattle."

He nodded. "That's certainly the biggest part of it. We've lost too many critters to rustlers. Now we need to work on replenishing the herd."

"So what exactly will we be looking for?" I asked.

"Two cows to breed, if we can get them. We've got a fine bull who could use some extra work. Also one or two calves. We'll see what's available."

"Sounds like a plan," I said. "And what's the rest of the mission?"

He laughed. "It's actually something you can help with, if you're so inclined."

I turned to face him. "I suppose that depends on exactly what kind of help you want."

"It will involve sitting front and center, where we can get a good close look at every animal."

"What will we be looking for?"

"Brands," he said.

I thought back to what Walt Benson, the agricultural agent, had told me about branding. "I was under the impression branding wasn't done much anymore."

"That's correct," Lance said. "But we were among the last to discontinue the practice, and that was not so long ago. Many of our older animals have the Madonna brand. It's a pick and shovel crossed with the pick head and the shovel head on top."

That was easy enough to picture, but what he was saying still didn't make any sense. "You're not trying to tell me that the rustlers are stupid enough to attempt to sell an animal with the Madonna brand on it?"

"Good lord, no," he replied. "But a clever rustler could come up with a design to superimpose over the existing brand and turn it into something entirely different. Tricky, but it can be done."

I pondered that for a few moments. "So if any of the animals being auctioned are branded, we should check them out closely, right?"

"Right. And if anything looks the least bit suspicious, we'll bid on the critter. Also take a photo with your phone. Can do?"

"Can do." And doing so would mean I was actually working on my case.

AVENGING MADONNA

We were among the first to arrive in the auction hall, so were able to secure the seats we wanted. The place appeared ready to host a rodeo. It was arranged as an amphitheater, providing a reasonable view from pretty much anywhere. The stage area was good-sized, with a dirt floor and a podium in the center. The seats filled up quickly, mostly with middle-aged men in faded jeans and cowboy hats.

At precisely noon, two men appeared on the stage, both wearing fringed vests and ten-gallon hats. The taller of the two stepped up on the podium and removed his hat.

"Howdy, folks," he said. "Welcome to this week's auction. You all know how this works, so let's get down to business." Someone in the bleachers behind us shouted "Yee haw!"

A door in the back of the stage opened and a cow emerged. The other man on the stage prodded the animal with a whip to convince it to strut around and show its stuff. The fellow at the podium began speaking at warp speed. Apparently people were bidding, though quietly so. I never heard a thing. Then the action stopped, the room fell silent and the animal in question retreated through a second door. And a new one came out. From what I had followed of the proceedings, I might as well have been on another planet.

I noticed some electric signage on the wall behind the podium. It displayed some numbers, which seemed to change when the cattle did. "What's that?" I asked Lance, pointing as I spoke.

"Stats on the animal," he said. "Weight, vaccination info, things like that." He reached out and gently lowered my hand. "And, by the way, it's probably better not to point at things. Or you may end up buying a cow."

I decided to sit on my hands for the remainder of the auction and simply look for brands on animals. I'd only use my hands if I needed to take a picture.

Lance bid on several animals, making barely discernable gestures with his right hand. At the same time, he somehow managed to carry on a conversation with me. And he was very chatty.

"So how do you like the Madonna Ranch?" he asked. "Pretty nice group of fellows, don't you think?"

I agreed. "Jess and Rusty and Pickins have been particularly helpful. Also Clint."

"They always are. The four of them have been around forever. I don't know how the place would manage without them."

I forged on, curious to see what Lance could tell me about the others. "I wish I'd had a chance to know Gus. I've heard nothing but good things about him."

Lance nodded. "Gus was a great guy. A pleasure to work with. Also an experienced cowhand. Knew the grazing land like the back of his hand." He shook his head. "It doesn't make any sense that he fell the way he did. He knew the terrain better than that."

Exactly what I had been thinking. "Wasn't Brody supposed to be working with Gus that night? What do you suppose happened to him?"

"I suppose he was up to his usual shenanigans," Lance smirked. "Making time with the ladies when he should have been working out in the hills. He fancies himself a real ladies' man, you know."

I thought back to the photo the cowhands were passing around the other day, but decided not to mention it.

Lance continued, "Brody's latest conquest is Alexa, from the gift shop. It'll be interesting to see how long that lasts. From what I've heard about Alexa, she's a handful and a half."

I decided not to comment on that either.

"And then there's Huddleston," Lance said. "God rest his crazy soul. I liked the guy well enough, but he sure was an odd one."

"What do you mean?"

Lance screwed up his face as he thought. "Well, for one thing, he wasn't much of a cowhand. Worked at three other ranches in the area before coming to Madonna and didn't seem to have learned a thing at any of them. The dude wasn't interested in much of anything except that book he was writing. That and the gold he expected to find."

"Did you just say what I think you said? Don was looking for gold?"

"That's what he told me one night when he'd been drinking. Said he knew there was gold buried on the Madonna land and he was fixing to find it."

Bingo! Things started falling into place in my head. "Did you tell the sheriff about that?" I asked.

"Hell no. He would've thought I was as nutty as Don. Anyway, I figured it was just some crazy notion Huddleston came up with. No point in spreading it around."

No point indeed. "What about Frank?" I asked.

Lance rolled his eyes. "He's all right, I guess. Not one of my favorites."

Before I could pursue that topic, the auction came to a close.

"That's it," Lance said. "How about I drop you back at the inn? Then I've got to come back here and pay for the critters I bought."

"Sure." I could use the time to make notes on what I'd just learned and see what I could make of it all.

Lance hesitated. "Oh, and, um, one other thing."

"What's that?"

"Would you like to join me for dinner on Sunday?"

"That'd be nice." It would also be considered work, because I'd pick his brains about the goings-on at the ranch. So it wouldn't be cheating on Pete.

"Great. I'll pick you up at 6:00."

And maybe then you can tell me why Frank isn't one of your favorites.

Chapter 27

Some days things don't go as expected. And that's not necessarily a bad thing. I was barely in my room for ten minutes when the phone rang.

My friend the coroner.

"Amy, hi, Mike Griswold here, calling you from the coroner's office."

"Mike, what in the world are you doing working on a Saturday afternoon?" I asked, wondering if perhaps he didn't have anything better to do with his weekend.

He laughed. "I've been honoring the request of a certain lady. She asked me to take another look at something and I didn't want to let her down. Listen, can you come to my office today?"

"Does that mean you found something?"

"It does. And I can't explain it to you over the phone. You need to see it in person."

"I'll be right there."

Less than ten minutes later, I parked my rented Mustang in front of the coroner's office. Mike was waiting for me at the front door, grinning from ear to ear. "I'm so glad you could make it here today. I don't think I could have waited until Monday to show you what I found."

The look of excitement on his face was positively contagious. "Well, then, let's see it." I followed him into a large lab, happily devoid of anybody recently deceased.

He led me to the far side of the room. A soiled and threadbare denim jacket lay there on a table.

I made an educated guess. "The jacket Gus was wearing when he fell?"

Mike nodded. "The first time around, I didn't find anything of interest with it. Then I had an idea."

I waited for him to continue, fighting not to appear over-eager.

"I realized I hadn't checked it with luminol," he said.

"Isn't luminol used to detect blood stains?"

He nodded. "I didn't bother with it originally in Gus's case because, while the fall did result in some bleeding, it was limited to his head. His jacket wasn't stained or torn. It never occurred to me to check for other substances, particularly on his clothing. After our chat the other day, I got to thinking about the fact that luminol is able to detect other substances as well – certain bodily fluids in particular, but also copper, iron and a variety of toxins."

I nodded my understanding, impatient for the other shoe to drop. "What kind of toxins can it detect? Anything interesting?"

"There's a toxic oil called urushiol," he said. "It's derived from poison oak and poison ivy plants."

"And you found this on Gus's jacket?"

"Correct. But only in one spot on the back. The rest of the jacket was soiled and a little dusty. Then I found this. Right here" He applied some luminol to the back of the jacket, then held it up for me to see.

I checked it out. "It looks like a hand print."

"A glove, actually. A hand print would have been better, because we would be able to lift fingerprints from that. But we can still learn a few things from the glove."

I thought for a moment, then said, "The print is in the middle of the back of the jacket. That suggests to me that somebody, wearing gloves, had his hand on Gus's back."

"Exactly!"

"And that in turn suggests that perhaps Gus didn't trip into the ravine. He could have been pushed."

"That's how I'm reading this," Mike said. "It appears likely that Gus's death wasn't an accident after all. We are dealing with a murder."

Holy shit! "Did you tell the police?"

"That's next on my agenda. I thought I'd give you a heads-up first."

And I was glad he did. I took a few deep breaths as I mulled the situation over. "The fact that he didn't just trip into the ravine doesn't actually surprise me. From what I've heard about Gus, he was an experienced hand at Madonna. He knew the terrain and its risks. It seemed doubtful that he would make a rookie mistake, even at night."

"Agreed. The Gus I was acquainted with knew what he was doing."

I frowned as I contemplated where to go from there. "And my job from here on is to figure out who pushed him. And why." *And how it's somehow connected to the rustling.*

Mike sighed. "I can't help you with the why. But there may be a way to zero in on the who. At least to narrow it down a bit."

I plunked myself into a chair. "I'm all ears."

"Like I said earlier, the oil on the glove is derived from poison oak or poison ivy plants."

I finished the thought for him. "So whoever was wearing these gloves must have had contact with those plants."

"And poison oak is rampant in the hills in this part of California."

Good to know. "But why would anybody be touching it, even with gloves?"

"To remove it from the grazing areas. In large amounts, urushiol can be toxic to cattle."

"So somebody was pulling it up to protect the cattle. Common sense says it had to be somebody from the ranch. That certainly narrows down the list of suspects." And I was probably acquainted with all of them.

"How long does the oil remain transferable on the gloves?" That could help narrow the field of suspects.

"I'm not quite sure," he said. "Got to do a little research on that."

"Is it premature to go to the police with this?" I asked.

He nodded. "Not really. Even though we don't have more information about who was wearing those gloves recently. I wish you luck with that. At any rate, I'm happy I was able to be of help to you."

"I can't thank you enough. Actually, I could just hug you for it," I surprised myself by saying.

"And I could just let you," Mike replied.

I did so, then said good-bye as I planned my next move. I needed to speak with Jess. I called him from my car and gave him a brief summary of what I had just learned. And how I'd like to proceed.

He took it all fairly calmly. "Let me check a few things out on this end. I'll get back to you as soon as I know anything."

I couldn't ask for anything more. And couldn't wait to see what he might learn.

Chapter 28

My phone rang early Sunday morning. Caller ID announced Jess.

"Good morning," I said.

"And the same to you. Sorry to call so early, but I've got a busy day ahead of me and wanted to get back to you right away about that glove. Didn't want to keep you in suspense."

"That's great." *Let's hope it will identify Gus's killer.* I held my breath and grabbed a pen to make a note.

"The job of pulling poison oak out in the hills is rotated among all the ranch hands on a four-week basis," Jess said. "Nobody really wants to do it, so I do my best to be fair."

"That sounds like a good system," I said, with more patience than I was actually feeling.

"I checked the work schedule for the last two months."

"And who was on poison oak weeding duty recently, around the time that Gus died?"

"That'd be Frank. And just for the record, he wasn't one bit happy about it. He hated that assignment. Pissed and moaned something fierce. Felt he was meant to be doing bigger and better things."

Frank? Probably the ranch hand I knew the least about. The one thing I knew for sure was that Lance wasn't overly fond of him. But did this mean he actually pushed Gus into the ravine?

I thought it over for a few moments. "That's great to know, Jess." I said. "There's just one more question, if I may."

"Shoot."

"Where are those gloves kept when they're not being used?"

"On a hook in the barn."

"So anybody could have access to them at any time."

"Yup. I suppose so."

Bummer! "Thanks, Jess. This is hugely helpful. Have a good day."

I struggled between being disappointed that this information didn't positively point to Frank as Gus's killer and being pleased that the number of suspects had been reduced to people who might have gone into the barn. I'd figure it out soon, somehow or other.

I was headed to the shower when my phone rang again. This time it was Clint.

"Good morning, Amy," he said. "I thought I'd start your day out with some helpful news."

"Sounds good to me. What's up?"

"I got in touch with the lawyer who is handling one of the offers to buy the property."

"And?"

He sighed loudly. "And I'm not real proud of strong-arming him the way I did, but in the end he agreed to identify his clients. He wasn't real happy about it, but I had him over a barrel."

"Do I want to know the details of this proverbial barrel?" I asked.

"No, you do not."

That was a relief. "So who is it?"

"A fellow named Martinez. Roberto Martinez."

Aha! Interesting. I made a note. "Do you know this guy?"

"Can't place him," Clint says. "Martinez is a pretty common name around these parts."

It was also the last name of the original owners of the Madonna property, which included Elena the diarist and her son the highwayman. I never did believe in coincidences. There had to be a connection here. The trick now would be to find that connection.

"Thanks, Clint. I appreciate your help here, no matter how you managed to get it."

"My pleasure," he said. "I'm happy to help. Enjoy your day."

I smiled as I disconnected. Armed with these two new pieces of information, I believed I would indeed enjoy my day. I jumped in the shower, eager to mull things over and decide where to go from here.

It seemed that my popularity was at an all-time high today. Two messages arrived for me while I was in the shower – both voice mails, one from Peggy, the other from my boss Mark.

I opened Peggy's first.

"Good morning" it said. "Sorry to call so early, particularly on a Sunday, but I need to give you a heads-up. George is on the warpath yet again. He's mouthing off to anybody who will listen about how you're dragging your feet on the Madonna claim because you want a free vacation in California. I'm pretty sure Mark has heard it by now. I thought you might want advance notice so you can prepare your defense."

I silently thanked her for the heads-up.

"George is also assigning all manner of petty jobs to Tiffany. I believe he's trying to tie up her time as much as possible so that I'm flying solo here. Pain in the ass. Not to worry about that, though. I've got things all under control. Just beware of George. And probably expect to hear from Mark. No need to call me back. I'll be out and about the rest of the day. Catch you tomorrow or so."

Interesting, though not a surprise. George had been my nemesis at the office ever since the day I got promoted over him. It had been an uphill battle for ages now. I was pretty sure I was winning it.

Peggy was spot-on about the message from Mark.

His tone was measured and firm, a far cry from when he was acting as my best friend's husband rather than my boss.

"I don't usually do business on a Sunday, but today is an exception, a very big exception. We need to take care of this Madonna business," he said. "It's been over a week now since the claim was filed. From what I read in the notes, it's a relatively small loss. That means we simply cannot afford to put a lot of time into it. You know, I was happy to send you out there to deal with things in person. The Madonnas are a long-time valued client. I did, however, expect you to be able to wrap it up within a few days." I held my breath, worried what he'd say next.

I held my breath, worried what he'd say next.

"Is there a problem I haven't heard about?" he continued. "I certainly hope not. At any rate, please do whatever is necessary to put this claim to rest and get yourself back to the office as quickly as possible. Don't bother returning my call. I expect that our next conversation will be in person."

Mark only used that tone of voice when he was really, really pissed. The trouble was that he was right. And if I valued my job, I needed to get cracking and solve this mess fast. The question at this point was where and how. When was already decided. It had to be now.

Chapter 29

My immediate plan was to treat myself to a large breakfast. That way, I could skip lunch and work through the day before my dinner with Lance. As I filled my face with delicious hot grease, aka bacon, eggs and home fries, I worked on my plan of attack.

The answer was obvious. I needed to know the history of the Martinez family that had owned the Madonna land. I had seen a history museum up the street from the old mission church. That was the logical place to start. I swallowed the last of my coffee and headed toward my car.

The museum was located in an attractive old red brick building. They were just opening when I arrived a few minutes after 11:00. An older, bookish looking man greeted me at the door. He had snowy white hair, a pleasant smile that continued all the way to his eyes and a sturdy wooden cane to steady himself.

"Hello," he said. "Please, come in. You're our first visitor on this beautiful Sunday. I'm Virgil Matthews, docent and local historian."

"It's nice to meet you."

"Is there anything in particular I can do for you? Or do you prefer simply to browse?"

AVENGING MADONNA

I liked a man who got straight to the point. "I recently read a book about the history of San Luis Obispo County and I'd like to know more. I can't believe how brutal it was. How lawless."

He nodded. "That's for sure. Back in the day, life was pretty violent around here. Highwaymen, vigilantes, villains of every sort. You name it, we had it. Lots of killing, hangings, and semi-legal shenanigans. Precious few reprisals. There was no real law to speak of. Chaos reigned supreme."

"That's hard to imagine nowadays," I said. "We seemed to have evolved somewhat as a species."

"One can hope," he replied.

"I was particularly fascinated by the story of Diego Martinez," I said. "Father Felipe at the mission church told me the story of how he became a highwayman to avenge the death of his wife."

"A very sad story, indeed. Also quite typical of the times."

"As I understand it, Diego was part of the Martinez family that originally owned the Madonna land."

Matthews nodded. "Quite right. And back in those days, life was all about the land. The ranchers became rich during the gold rush. Everybody wanted a piece of the action. A lot of blood was shed by people defending their land."

"What can you tell me about the Martinez family? Were they the original owners of the ranch land?"

"Correct. The Martinez ranch dates back to long before California became a part of the United States. At the time of the gold rush, it was owned by Guillermo Martinez and his wife Elena. They had several children who worked the ranch with them. Diego was the exception, preferring to make his living by other means."

"Father Felipe mentioned something to me about a feud concerning ownership of the Martinez land. What can you tell me about that?"

A small sad smile dashed across the docent's face. "That was probably the worst of the land feuds. And the one which lasted the longest. As the story goes, a fellow named Henry Goff coveted the Martinez land. He set out to get it by any means necessary."

"What did he do?" I asked.

"He began with the obvious – offering to buy the place. When that didn't work, he resorted to more hostile means. Threats, allegedly accidental fires at buildings on the property. Stolen cattle. Damage to the outbuildings and the crops. Nothing worked. Eventually he blocked off the access roads to the property, hoping to starve the Martinez family out. That's when Guillermo began to take him seriously."

"How so?" I asked.

The docent shook his head. "This is where things become a bit muddy. There are two distinct versions of what happened next. I don't know for sure which of them is accurate. If you have time, I can elaborate on that."

Good grief. I had all the time in the world for this guy. He was a veritable fountain of information. "I'd like that."

Matthews indicated two chairs on the other side of the room. "How about we have a seat and I'll tell you what I can?"

Good idea.

We sat. He continued, "It seems that Guillermo Martinez and Henry Goff were both big drinkers as well as avowed gamblers. One version of the story says that Martinez, now nearly broke, agreed to a poker game, with the land going to the winner. He was taking a big risk here. One must assume that he had little choice. To nobody's surprise, Goff won. Martinez accused him of cheating."

I clenched my pen with cramped fingers, scolding myself for not thinking to record the conversation on my phone. *Oh well, I'll remember next time.*

"The other version says that Goff forged Martinez's signature on a bill of sale ceding the land to Goff. Martinez knew nothing about it until he discovered someone surveying the land for Goff. Martinez protested to the local authorities, such as they were, but with no luck. The deed to the land was now in Goff's name."

"Which story do you believe?" I asked.

He shook his head. "I suppose we'll never know for sure. I like the romance, the randomness of the card game. But I do have trouble believing Martinez would do anything that rash. Whichever story is true, the end result was a shoot-out in the middle of town. Goff shot Martinez, who died immediately. Martinez's son Juan then shot Goff, who also died. Juan was tried for murder and hanged."

"And the Goff family took over the ranch?" I asked.

"Over the protests of Elena Martinez and her remaining children. They were forced off the land but always remained in the area. A blood feud ensued which lasted for generations – with bad feelings all around. For a very long time."

"Why did the Goff family eventually sell?"

"The most recent owner, Henry Goff IV, was an artist who had no interest in ranching. He was happy to sell the land to anybody other than the Martinez descendants."

"That was when Alex Madonna bought the land in 1950, right?"

Matthews nodded. "The hope is that the story, and the feud, both ended there."

I had a feeling that wasn't exactly so. Thanking the docent for his time and information, I stood and made ready to leave. Then I noticed something on the wall by the door. There was an old photo, sepia colored, that bore a remarkable resemblance to the man I had seen arguing with Rosa outside the café the other day. "Any idea who that is?" I asked.

"Sorry. No idea."

I had an idea. Now I just needed to figure out how to prove it and where to go from there. I said a silent prayer that my dinner with Lance might help me find the way.

Chapter 30

I was looking forward to my dinner with Lance. This, of course, meant that I had also been feeling more than a little guilty about it. Mark's message changed all that. Lance was now more important to my case. He knew cattle ranching. He knew the ranch hands at Madonna. My gut told me he wasn't involved in the rustling himself, but he may be able to help me figure out who was. It was worth my while to pick his brain. And the sooner the better.

A call from Pete came through while I was changing my clothes. I chose to ignore it for the time being. No sense letting guilt spoil my evening. I'd deal with that tomorrow.

Lance knocked on my door ten minutes earlier than expected. That meant I didn't have a chance to pop into the bathroom before we left. Oh well, I was pretty sure it could wait until we got to the restaurant, as long as it wasn't too far away.

"You look nice," he said as he eyed my denim skirt, white turtle neck and soft pink shawl – the closest I could come to western dress.

He looked nice as well, but I kept that to myself. That was tough. Lance was more than attractive and I was far from immune to his charms. But it was better not to encourage the guy. I'd be going home to Pete in a few days.

AVENGING MADONNA

Once we were in his truck and on our way, Lance said, "We're heading over to Morro Bay. It's only about a dozen miles from here. I thought you might like to see a little more of this area than just San Luis Obispo. Morro Bay's a nice town. There are a couple of excellent seafood restaurants right on the water. I made us a reservation at the Galley Bar and Grill. The food is great there, and the view is even better."

That sounded good to me.

We weren't on the road ten minutes when the rain began – with a vengeance. By the time we reached Morro Bay, it was pouring something fierce.

"So much for an ocean view while we dine," Lance said. "How about I drop you off at the door so you don't get drenched? I'll park the car then run like heck through the raindrops."

"That'd be great. I'll use the time to pop into the Ladies' Room."

"Meet you in the lobby," he said.

The Ladies' Room was just off the lobby. I headed for the stall furthest from the door. They tended to be the cleanest. I hadn't even locked the door when I heard someone enter the room. Two women, laughing and talking. I recognized one of the voices as Rosa from the coffee shop at the inn. The other was most likely her sister Alexa.

I was now faced with two choices: cough or make some other sound so they'd know there was somebody else in the room or gather my knees up to my chest so they wouldn't see my feet under the door.

I chose not to cough, hoping I might overhear something of interest.

I heard a stall door shut. Luckily it wasn't the one next to me. Some days you just live right. "I'll be quick," Rosa said.

"Don't rush," came the reply. "I don't mind waiting. I need to fix my make-up anyway. That rain made a real mess of it."

"Then the celebration can begin," said Rosa from the stall. "Lord knows we've waited long enough for it."

Alexa turned on a faucet. I strained to hear their conversation over the sound of running water. "After all this time, I can't believe it's nearly over," she said. "We'll finally get back what is rightfully ours. And then they can all go straight to Hell. Particularly that ass Brody. Lord knows I'm sick of romancing the guy just to keep him distracted and away from Gus in the hills at night."

Rosa laughed. "I was surprised you didn't end it right after Gus died."

"I'm working on it," was the reply.

"And then there's that damn fool Don. It sure was lucky that he liked his liquor, then couldn't control his mouth. Good thing Frank was drinking with him, not one of the other ranch hands."

"That's for damn sure. Too bad he didn't live long enough for us to thank him." Alexa said.

Rosa snorted. "The world is well rid of him. We better get back to the party now. We don't want to miss anything."

They both laughed. Then the sound of the hand dryer muffled anything else they may have said.

I finished my business – and not a moment too soon – then waited for what seemed like forever to be very sure they left the room before I ventured out of my stall. I took my time washing my hands as well, so Alexa and Rosa woud be gone before I ventured into the lobby.

Lance was waiting by the hostess station. "There you are," he said. "Our table is ready." We followed the hostess into the dining room.

Lance glanced around the dining room when we entered. I followed his gaze to a table on his right. And there sat four people – Rosa, Alexa, Frank the cowhand and another fellow I recognized as the guy I saw arguing with Rosa the other day. The one who looked like the photo in the museum.

"Well I'll be," Lance said. "If it isn't the Martinez family. Fancy running into you folks here."

AVENGING MADONNA

Martinez? Their name is Martinez? I struggled to retain my composure as my brain catapulted into overdrive. Doing my best to sound casual, I said. "Rosa, I thought I recognized your voice in the ladies' room just now."

A look of panic shot across Rosa's face. Alexa's mouth fell open. Nobody at their table spoke.

I continued, "Your last name is Martinez? Wow. I didn't know that. Are you descendants of Elena Martinez? I learned about her from the priest at the mission church. Pretty interesting story."

Still no response.

Lance filled the awkward silence by saying, "So, Rob, when did you get paroled?"

The guy who was apparently Rob ignored the question. He said, "Howdy, Lance. You still in the area?"

The hostess cleared her throat with an impatient sound. "This way, please, folks."

Lance ignored her and grinned at Rob. "Never left town. I'm glad I stuck around long enough to see the entire Martinez family together again." With that, he turned away and followed the hostess to a table for two on the opposite side of the room.

Lance lowered his voice and said, "Is this making you uncomfortable? Do you want to go somewhere else?"

"Hell no. Let's make them uncomfortable." I pointed to two tables in the center of the room, both occupied by parties of six, everyone having a raucous good time. "I doubt we could overhear the Martinez clan given the noise level in this room, but that works both ways. Let's keep looking their way and pointing to them off and on – just to make sure they know we're talking about them. I have a lot of questions for you."

He grinned. "At your service. But perhaps we should order first."

Chapter 31

I waited until my wine and Lance's beer were served and our meals were ordered before beginning my inquisition.

"The Martinez family?" I began. "They're all related?"

"Well, yeah. You didn't know?" he said.

"I knew Rosa and Alexa were sisters. Didn't know Frank was their brother. Never mind the other guy. And I had no idea their name was Martinez."

Lance stopped me there. "Actually, it isn't any more. All four of them changed their names several years ago. I only used it just now to piss them off."

I grinned at him. "I think it worked. Do you have any idea why they would bother to change their name?"

Lance shook his head. "Not exactly. My best guess is that they were trying to distance themselves from that damn old feud."

"With the Goff family?" I asked.

Lance's eyes grew wise with surprise. "How the heck do you know about that?"

"I heard about it in the history museum just this morning. From what the docent said, it apparently went on for a lot of years, generations even."

"If you say so," Lance shrugged. "I never really paid much attention to all that. Guess I was too busy just being a kid."

Our appetizers arrived – crab cakes for me, clam chowder for Lance. All conversation ceased as we both dug in. I strained to overhear the conversation from the Martinez table, but with no luck. Instead I worked on piecing together what I knew, or could guess, about the Martinez clan.

After a few tasty bites, I asked Lance, "Can we back up here for a minute?"

"Sure."

"How do you know the Martinez family?"

"Grew up with them. San Luis Obispo was smaller back then. Everybody knew everybody. The Martinez kids were always a bunch of hot heads. Seemed like there was bad blood between them and the rest of the world. Their parents were the same way. Still can't figure out why. They were nothing special from what I could see."

"Was it awkward working with Frank at the ranch?"

Lance sighed. "I suppose so. Just did my best when I had to work with him and ignored him the rest of the time."

I sat and listened to Lance, wishing I had remembered to record this on my phone. I didn't want to miss a word of this.

"So what about the other brother? He's been in jail?" I asked.

"Federal prison, actually. Bank robbery. Must have got out early for good behavior, or some such horse shit. Oops. Excuse the language."

"Not a problem."

The waitressed delivered our dinners, scallops for me, steak for Lance. I took a break from my questioning long enough to enjoy my meal. During that time, and barely noticed by me, the dining room cleared out considerably. Which meant that the noise level dropped.

The Martinez siblings appeared not to be aware of the decrease in the decibel level. They were busy laughing and toasting themselves.

I tuned in.

"Nice going, folks," Bob said. "Here's to a job well done."

"That's for damn sure," Rosa replied. "It's been a long, hard road, but we're almost there."

"It's about goddam time," Bob said. "But it'll be well worth the wait."

"And here's to our good friend Don," Frank added. "We couldn't have done it without him."

"Such a shame he couldn't be here to celebrate with us," Bob said. Everybody laughed.

The four of them raised their glasses. Someone said, "To us!" The others echoed the sentiment. Someone added "And to our land."

Rosa glanced across the room, her eyes settling on me and Lance, as if suddenly remembering we were there. Lance winked at me. He flashed a big smile at Rosa, raised his glass to her and nodded.

She scowled in return. "Come on, guys. Time to get out of here. We've still got a lot to do. And nobody is going to stop us now." Her eyes shot daggers in my direction as she rose to leave.

A shiver ran down my spine as I watched the Martinez clan leave the dining room. Rosa sent one last glance my way. Was that a threat?

Chapter 32

The police telephoned me first thing the next morning, disturbing what had been a restless night. They wanted me to come in to discuss the discovery of Don's body with them - at 10:00 sharp.

I told them sure, no problem, then set about mentally rearranging my day. The plan had been to ride out in the hills with Pickins. Per home office standard procedures, I needed to see, and document, the scenes of the crimes, aka the rustling or slaying of cattle, then close the claim and set it up for payment. And I needed to do it all ASAP if I wanted to keep my job.

I dressed quickly, downed a cup of coffee and walked to the ranch office to reschedule my ride with Pickins. As important as this was for me, sometimes there are other priorities. Today the San Luis Obispo police took precedence.

"You're a mite early," Pickins greeted me, "but no problem. I'll just saddle up a couple of horses and we can be on our way."

I shook my head. "Sorry. We're going to have to put this off until later. I've been summoned to meet with the police this morning. They want to question me about finding Don Huddleston's body. Can we postpone our ride until this afternoon?"

"I'm afraid not," Pickins replied. "The cops called me as well. They want me there at 1:30. By the time I get back from that, it'd be too late to head out into the hills with you. Days are getting shorter, you know. Better we shouldn't be out there after dark. Can we do it tomorrow?"

This was not good news. I frowned as I considered my options. "You know," I told him, "There's actually no reason you need to come with me on this ride."

Pickins shook his head. "I'd love to say I could send somebody else with you, but we're short-handed at the moment. And we've got a lot to get done today. Can't spare anyone at least until tomorrow."

"Unfortunately I can't wait until then," I told him. "I'm getting pressure from my boss to finish my business here and get back to the office as quickly as possible. I need to get this done today. I can go by myself."

He stared at me wide-eyed. "I don't know about that. I am responsible for your safety you know. Can't have you taking chances being out there all by yourself."

"I'll be fine. I've had plenty of experience riding. Just give me a gentle horse and a map to help me find my way around. I'm sure you let other guests ride out without a guide."

"We do," he admitted with a sigh. "Can't say that I like the idea, but I guess I can't stop you. I'll have a mount saddled up and waiting for you. A very gently mount."

"Thanks."

"Now we better talk about this map. Where exactly do you want to go? What do you need to see?"

I thought for a moment. "I'd like to ride the outlying areas of the property, looking for places where a truck could pull in easily, or be parked out of sight. I'll also need to see where the cattle were grazing before they went missing. And the places where they were found dead."

"That easy," Pickins said. "I'll draw a map up and mark those locations for you."

"There's no real need for me to revisit the place where you and I found Don's body. The police tape is probably still up there but that doesn't matter because I already took photos of it." *And the vision of it is forever etched in my mind.*

"Right."

"I should also take a look at the spot where Gus fell to his death. Something tells me that is somehow related to the rustling problem."

"Gotcha," Pickins said. "Is that it?"

"I believe it is."

"I'll draw this up and have it ready and waiting for you. And I wish you luck. Be sure to be back before sundown. And promise me you'll be careful."

"That is always my intention," I said. "No need to worry about me." I sent that thought out to the universe, hoping that would help to make it so.

Chapter 33

I arrived a few minutes early for my appointment with the local police. Rather than appear over-eager, I sat in the car and reviewed my investigation notes and the photos I had taken at the scene of Don Huddleston's demise. It couldn't hurt for me to arrive prepared.

"Good morning," I said as I entered the station a few minutes later. "My name is Amy Lynch. I have a meeting with Officer Daniels."

"Right," the desk sergeant replied. "He's expecting you." He pointed to a hallway behind him. "Second door on the left."

Daniels was waiting for me by the door. "Hello, Ms. Lynch. We appreciate you coming in to see us. Please have a seat. I promise I'll make this as quick and painless as I can."

I sat. "I'm happy to help. What can I tell you?"

He referred to his notes. "Let's see. You were one of the two people who found Mr. Huddleston's body, correct?"

"Yes."

"What were you doing out in the hills?"

"I wanted to get a good look at all of the Madonna land," I told him.

He rolled his eyes ever so slightly. "Whatever for?"

"To see the locations where some of the cattle had gone missing, or been killed."

He nodded. "Yeah. Right. I remember hearing something about some rustling going on there. But why did you want to check that out? Aren't you a guest at the inn? What's your interest in missing cattle?"

"I'm an investigator for the company that insures the Madonnas. I'm here to settle the claim for the lost cattle."

He made a note. "And while riding in the hills with Mr. Pickins, you came upon the body of Mr. Huddleston?"

"That's correct. We noticed some vultures circling the area and went to investigate."

"Tell me what you saw when you got there."

I struggled to contain my inner grimace. It was a sight I would never forget. "I can do better than tell you," I said. "I can show you." I grabbed my cell phone and pulled up the photos I had taken.

Daniels scrolled slowly through the photos, grunting a few times. He handed me back my phone and said, "Not much left of the poor guy. How did you know it was Huddleston?"

"Pickins recognized a rather distinctive ring Don used to wear."

"I see," He paused and appeared to be lost in thought for a moment. "How well did you know Mr. Huddleston?"

"I never met him."

"Hmmm. So I'm guessing you don't know much about him then."

"I may know more than you'd think," I said.

He gave me an odd look. "And why is that?"

"I had my office run a background check on all of the cowhands. That's standard practice in any investigation."

"And what did this standard background check tell you about Mr. Huddleston?"

I checked my notes from what Peggy had told me. "He's originally from Philadelphia. Has a BA in history from Pennsylvania State University. He minored in creative writing."

Daniels looked up from his notes. "And he was working as a cowhand?"

"Yes. He worked at three other ranches in the San Luis Obispo area before landing at Madonna. He had been there a few years now."

"Do you find that odd?" Daniels asked. "I mean, a fellow with that much education working on a ranch?"

"I did at first," I admitted. "Until I learned something else about him."

"And what was that?"

"He was also a writer. He had two books published. Both non-fictions."

"I'm assuming this is pertinent," he said. "What were they about?"

"His hobby," I responded, dragging out my final revelation. I couldn't help myself. I enjoyed creating a dramatic effect, however minor.

Daniels gave me an impatient glare. "Which was?"

"He was a treasure hunter."

"Well I'll be darned," Daniels said. "We don't see too much of that around here. What the heck kind of treasure did he expect to find in the Madonnas's hills?"

"Gold."

"Gold? You putting me on? Why in the world would anybody expect to find gold out there?"

I proceeded to fill Daniels in on what I knew about Diego Martinez and family. Also what I had read in Elena's diary and the book I had bought on local history.

Daniels gave me a funny look. "I guess I should have paid more attention in history class, or to local legends," he said. "And you believe all this to be true?"

"I have no reason not to. Elena's diary certainly appeared to be authentic. And Father Felipe at the mission seemed to believe it as well."

After some thought, Daniels said, "Let me see those pictures again."

I handed him my phone. I had a good idea where he was headed but decided to let him get there on his own.

He held up one shot for me to see. "So here's the shallow grave where the coyotes had their way with Huddleston."

I nodded.

He continued, "Then there's this other hole. It's bigger than Huddleston's grave. And a whole lot deeper. We didn't pay much attention to it at the time. Too busy moving the body. But now I'm getting to wonder about it."

I finished the thought for him. "Do you mean who dug this hole? And what was in it? And was it dug before or after Don was killed?"

"Yup. That about covers it. If what you're telling me is true, it's looking like maybe somebody found the gold."

"Exactly."

"Who do you suppose it was?" he asked me.

That was easy. "The descendants of Elena and Diego Martinez."

Daniels furrowed his brow. "Far as I know, there aren't any more Martinez descendants left in town."

"There actually are. Four of them. They've all changed their names. And they've been trying to buy the property from Mrs. Madonna."

He put down his note pad and pen. "And how did you come to know all this?"

I told him what I had overheard in the ladies' room. And also what Lance had told me.

"Son of a bitch," he said. "Looks like I'll be needing to have a talk with these folks. And the sooner the better."

I hoped against hope that I would be there to hear that conversation.

Chapter 34

I grabbed a fast-food burger on my way back to the inn. Eating in the Copper Café wasn't an option today. The last thing I needed, or wanted, was to come face to face with Rosa - at least not until I had a few issues resolved. And skipping lunch was definitely not an option for me - not today, probably not ever.

Back in my room, I changed into jeans, sneakers and a sweatshirt and headed out to the ranch. It was a wonderful day for a walk, bright and sunny, with just enough nip in the air to remind you that it was late October.

I smiled as I arrived at the corral by the barn. The sign "If you like your ride, kiss your horse and tip your guide" just tickled me. Two horses were saddled and waiting for riders. I hoped that both got kisses before the day was over.

Brody emerged from the ranch office. "Howdy. How you doing today?"

"Just fine, thanks," I told him. "I realize I'm a little early, but I'd like to get going now if that's not a problem."

"That's actually a good thing," he said. "I've got a doctor's appointment this afternoon and I don't want to be late."

I looked around. "Where is everybody? Are you all alone here until Pickins gets back?"

"Rusty and Lance are out on the range this morning." He glanced around the yard. "Frank's here someplace. Don't see him at the moment."

After last night, that was just fine with me.

"I'll run inside and grab the map Pickins left for you," Brody said.

He was back in a flash. "This all looks pretty straight-forward. You shouldn't have any trouble with it."

"Thanks."

Brody frowned. "Are you sure you want to go out there alone? You know, if you waited until tomorrow, either Pickins or Lance could ride with you."

I shook my head as I mounted the horse. "Sorry. I really need to get this done today."

"Well then, have a good ride."

Off I rode, map in hand, heading toward the grazing areas. On this sun-filled day, the land was beautiful in a stark sort of way. The grassland was dry and occasionally broken by low shrubs and rock formations. I took my time, enjoying the gentle breeze, yet also trying to concentrate on my mission. I needed to document evidence of rustling and also come up with suggestions for increased security to prevent future problems.

"Hello there," a voice interrupted my thoughts.

I turned my head to see Lance and Rusty heading my way on horseback.

"Lovely day for a ride," Rusty said.

Lance added, "Are you sure you should be out here alone?"

"No choice," I told him. "This is more business than pleasure. And it can't wait another day."

"That's too bad," Lance said. "I'd love to be able to join you. Trouble is we've got a repair job back at the inn that requires both of us. Please tell me you have your phone with you, just in case you need it."

I held it up to show him.

"OK, then," he said. "Enjoy your ride. Just be careful out there."

They rode off toward the inn.

I headed to the hills, glancing at the map off and on as I rode. The occasional steer greeted me along the way. They sure were good sized creatures, and not a bit shy of humans. They were also noisier than I expected.

I thought I heard another sound as well, a faint whistling somewhere in the distance. I shrugged it off, figuring it was probably just the wind in the hills.

Reaching the outer boundaries of the Madonna land, I pulled out my phone so I could document the area with both photos and voice memos.

The first thing I saw was that Pete had called again. Oh dear! I hadn't yet listened to his message from last night. Was I too wrapped up in my investigation to deal with him? Or was I avoiding him for other reasons? Good questions. No answers.

I filmed a few panoramic views of the hills, commenting on what, according to Pickens's map, had happened and where and how the cattle had probably been spirited away.

I spent as little time as possible at the site of Don Huddleston's demise. Just enough to confirm that it fit where Diego told Elena he buried the gold: *'Out in the hills, by your grandfather's unmarked grave below the twisted sycamore tree.* A twisted tree was there. Sure looked like a sycamore to me.

No need to stay here long. I had already photographed this area in detail for the police.

My final stop would be the ravine where Gus had met his death. As I prepared to get back onto my horse, a medium sized dog – some sort of German shepherd mix - approached me. His tail was wagging and I was pretty sure he was giving me the canine version of a smile.

I bent down to pat his head. "Hello, Buddy. Nice to see you. What are you doing out here all by yourself? Are you lost?"

He wagged his tail again and licked my face.

I thought of Sam and realized how much I missed him. It would be good to get back home to him. In the meantime, there was work to do.

"Time for us to go, Buddy. We need to finish this job quickly and return to some semblance of civilization."

I got back on my horse and headed off toward the ravine. My new friend followed. As I rode away, I thought I heard a horse snort in the distance. Or perhaps it was a steer chatting with his fellow cattle. I was certain they communicated with each other somehow. The dog heard it too and turned in the direction of the sound.

It was a short ride to the spot where Gus had fallen. As I prepared to dismount, I heard the soft whistling sound again. Definitely not the wind. A chill went up my spine.

The dog let out a long, low growl. Was it a threat or a warning? Or perhaps both? I jerked my head around to see what had caught his attention.

And there was Frank Martinez, leading a horse and walking slowly toward me – pointing a gun in my direction.

Chapter 35

"Stay right where you are," he snarled at me. "And don't try anything fancy."

I froze in place.

"And give me that phone," he added. "No way you're gonna be calling for help." He grabbed the phone from my hand.

The dog growled again, a louder, more menacing sound this time. He bared his teeth and began to walk toward Frank.

Frank aimed his gun at the dog and pulled the trigger, hitting my canine friend in the leg. The dog cried out in pain and collapsed.

I got down from my horse and started in the dog's direction to help him.

"I said don't move," Frank shouted. "Or I'll do the same to you. Or maybe worse."

I glared at Frank with my arms folded across my chest. What he didn't know was that I did this so he wouldn't how badly my hands were shaking. "Go ahead and try," I told him. "You're obviously not much of a shot."

Frank relaxed the gun in his hand. "Wouldn't waste a bullet on you anyway. There are other ways for you to die. Better ways."

"You mean being pushed into the ravine like Gus?" I asked.

"Something like that," he said. "Actually, you're going to jump. It will look like an accident. You probably went too close to the edge. The ground's pretty uneven up here. It would be easy for you to lose your balance, like Gus did. And you must have slipped. You get the picture? Now turn around."

I resisted his suggestion. No way I was going anywhere without a fight. Hands on my hips, I glared at Frank with far more bravado than I actually felt. "That's not going to happen," I told him. "There's no way in Hell you'll get away with it."

He made a sound somewhere between a laugh and a snort. "You sure about that?"

"You bet. I met with the police just this morning. Told them all about what your family has been up to. And why. They'll be questioning you any time now. And there's no way they'll buy the idea that I slipped. Not with what they know now about Gus's death, and Don's."

I needed to keep Frank talking – at least until I figured out what I could do to stay alive. "So, tell me, why did you kill Gus anyway? Really, what was the point? What did he do to you?"

Frank shrugged. "The guy was getting too suspicious, too close to figuring out how we were pulling off the rustling."

"You mean like having Alexa romance Brody in the hills at night to keep him distracted? And to prevent him from doing his job?"

An ugly smirk appeared on Frank's face. "Worked, didn't it? At least for a while. Kept Brody from doing his share of the work. And when Gus figured out what was going on, he got pissed being stuck with all the work while Brody was busy romancing Alexa."

"But like you said, that only worked for a while," I pointed out.

Frank grunted. "Because that damn fool was stupid enough to mention it to Alexa. To warn her to stay away, or he'd say something to Jess about what was going on."

The dog whimpered again. Frank turned toward him, gun in hand.

"And what about Don?" I asked in an effort to distract Frank from the dog. "Why did he have to die?"

"Let's just say he outlived his usefulness."

"How so?"

"First off the guy was stupid enough to get drunk and tell people he was hunting for gold. Most of them thought he was just nuts. I knew better. Me and Rob, we watched Don like hawks. Let him do all the leg work. Kept tabs on him until he actually found the gold. As soon as we saw him digging it up, we did away with him. That gold was ours. We weren't about to share it with him."

"The gold was on Madonna land," I reminded him. "Which means you actually stole it."

He grunted by way of reply.

"And, just for the record, where is that gold now?"

"None of your damn business," he snarled.

Whatever. I'd find it eventually, if I lived that long. Something occurred to me. "But why did you bury him in a shallow grave when there was already a deeper hole nearby?"

Frank shrugged. "That hole may have been deep, but it wasn't big enough. We would have had to bury him standing up."

I had no response to that. I looked around the hills, hoping to come up with another way to distract Frank. Or to get away from him somehow.

Nothing came to mind.

"You know," Frank said, "If you hadn't stuck your nose into our business, we wouldn't be here now."

"This *is* my business," I said. "I came here to settle the rustling claim." Not that it mattered at this point, but talking about it might buy me a few extra moments of life.

"OK. We're done talking," Frank growled. "Now you will please turn around and walk to the edge here. And don't try anything funny."

AVENGING MADONNA

Funny was the farthest thing from my mind. I stood my ground, defying him with every fiber of my being. And definitely not turning to face the ravine. "Not likely."

"Move," Frank snarled. He put his free hand on my shoulder and shoved, spinning me around and pushing me ever closer to the rim. I tried to push back. It didn't work. I held my breath, knowing that one more push would send me to my death. Gus was lucky, I thought. At least he never saw it coming.

Suddenly the dog barked. I heard horses galloping somewhere nearby. Hopefully someone – anyone – coming to my rescue.

Frank became distracted for a moment, turning his head toward the sound. I heard a bang. Had he decided to shoot me after all? But I didn't feel anything. I closed my eyes and said a silent prayer. Then something solid brushed against my shoulder, knocking me off balance. My arms flew up in an effort to keep me from pitching forward. I fought to steady myself. I opened my eyes and saw Frank's body free-falling past me without a sound into the very death trap he had intended for me.

Then two strong hands grabbed me and pulled me back from the brink. I spun around to see Pete's half-terrified, half-relieved eyes locked onto mine He pulled me close to him in the best hug I'd ever felt. I clung to him like my life depended on it. I cried, but they were tears of joy and relief.

Then I looked over Pete's shoulder and saw Lance about a dozen feet back, his smoking gun still pointed at the spot where Frank had last stood. "Happy landing," he said, apparently to Frank. "Couldn't have happened to a nicer guy."

Chapter 36

"What are you doing here?" I gasped.

"Saving your life," Pete said, "with the help of my new friend Lance." He led me to a rock formation away from the rim of the ravine. "You need to sit down. You look like you're about to collapse."

He was right about that.

"Nearly dying can do that to a person," I said. "And I thank you both for preventing that. But how did you find me?"

Pete pointed to Lance, who was a few feet away talking on the phone. "I was lucky enough to run into this guy."

Lance pocketed his phone and joined us. "The police are on their way. They want us to stay here so they can question us."

"And I suggest you use that time to tell me exactly how you knew I was here and needed help," I told them. "Start from the beginning and don't leave anything out."

Pete began. "Things finally quieted down at the office. I was feeling badly that I hadn't been able to come with you in the first place. I decided to surprise you. Thought we could spend a few days out here, then fly home together."

That sounded fine so far, and very much like my Pete.

"I got here a little while ago," he continued. "And went to the reception desk to ask for your room number. An older fellow came in at the same time."

"Pickens," Lance said.

"Right. And when he heard your name, he told me you weren't in your room. You were out riding the range. He said he expected you'd be back sometime soon and suggested I join him at the corral to wait for you. We walked out there and found Lance tending horses."

"I thought you and Rusty were out doing repairs," I said to Lance.

"So did Pickens," he replied. "He asked me why I was at the ranch and Frank wasn't."

"Good question," I said.

"I had gone to the barn to pick up a few tools Rusty and I needed. When Frank saw me there, he said an emergency had just come up and he had to leave. Asked if I could I take charge of things at the ranch until Pickens got back. I said sure. Frank jumped on a horse and took off like a shot."

"Which way was he headed?" I asked.

"Out toward the hills. Right where I had seen you heading earlier."

"But Frank didn't know I was out here."

Lance shook his head. "Apparently he did. Must have overheard you making plans with Pickens. Or maybe Brody."

"Son of a bitch," I said.

Lance continued, "And after last night, and the things we overheard at the restaurant, I knew you were in trouble. Frank considered you a threat."

"So he decided to deal with me the same way he had with Gus and Don."

"We weren't about to let that happen," Pete said.

Lance nodded. "That's for darn sure. I grabbed a gun, saddled up a couple of horses and Pete and I rode like hell."

"And got here just in time," I said, then turned to Pete. "I didn't know you knew how to ride a horse."

He grinned. "I was on the polo team at Yale."

The sound of approaching sirens put an end to our conversation. I took a deep breath and summoned every bit of inner strength I had. There was no time to fall apart now. I steeled myself to deal with the police once again.

Chapter 37

Several emergency vehicles arrived at once, sirens blaring and lights flashing. Officer Daniels, the fellow I had spoken with earlier in the day, jumped out of his cruiser and joined us by the edge of the ravine. After a brief assessment of the situation, he directed the other responders to the perimeter of the property where a dirt road wound down to the bottom of the ravine where Frank's body lay.

That done, he took note of Lance's presence and Pete's name, then turned to me. "Well, Ms. Lynch. Nice to see you again, and so soon."

"We've got to stop meeting like this," I replied. "Thanks for getting here so quickly."

"Just doing my job, Ma'am." He paused for a moment or two, then frowned. "You know, Ms. Lynch, I'm really glad you and I had that little chat this morning."

"Why is that?" I asked.

"Because otherwise I'd be getting mighty suspicious of you right about now."

"Whatever do you mean?" I did my best to sound sweet and innocent. Sometimes it works.

He drew in a deep breath. "Well, you've been in San Luis Obispo for just about a week now. And in that time, we've had three questionable deaths, all in the same general area. I'd be seeing some sort of connection here."

"Gus Delgado was already deceased when I arrived," I reminded him.

"At least that's what you say," he replied. "And after our talk this morning, I am inclined to believe you. You struck me as a basically honest person who is just doing her job.'"

That was a relief. I gave him what I hoped was a sincere and charming smile.

He returned the sentiment. "So, let's get on with this. How about you folks tell me what happened here today? I'm guessing it's related to the story Ms. Lynch told me this morning about the Martinez family and the buried gold."

I gave him a brief but thorough recap of my ordeal with Frank.

"That's quite a tale you tell," he said. "And based on what I'm seeing and hearing, there's no real reason to doubt your word. The question is, where do we go from here?"

Lance waved his hand in the officer's direction. "Can we begin by agreeing that Frank's death was the result of a righteous shooting on my part? It was obviously the only way to save Amy's life."

Daniels furrowed his brow in thought. "Can't argue with that. We'll chalk it up to justifiable homicide. After all, you do have witnesses to back it up."

"That's right," Pete said. "And if he hadn't shot the guy, I may just have done it myself."

A look of blessed relief lit up Lance's face.

"But what about the rest of it?" I asked. "Frank admitted to me that he and his siblings killed both Gus Delgado and Don Huddleston. And took the gold. They need to be prosecuted for all of that."

Daniels shook his head. "Sorry. That's not going to work."

"But why not?" I asked.

Pete decided to answer that. "It's all hearsay. It won't hold up in court." He turned to Daniels and added, "I'm an attorney."

Daniels nodded. "Good to know."

Pete was right, of course, but we couldn't just let things drop there. "So what can we do?" I asked Daniels. "We can't let the Martinez family get away with this. They murdered two people. And stole gold buried on Madonna land."

"We'll get to the gold in a bit," Daniels said. "Got to sort out these murders first. You've convinced me that the Martinez folks are most likely guilty here. The trouble is, the only actual forensic proof we have is against Frank for Gus's murder. Like your friend said, everything else is simply your account of what Frank told you."

I bit back my frustration and searched my brain for a solution.

And then it hit me, so hard and so fast that I almost did the classic heel of hand to forehead "oh dopey me" gesture. "Wait a minute folks. That may not be so. There's a chance we may have all the proof we need."

All eyes turned in my direction. Nobody said a word.

"On my phone," I told them.

"Your phone?" Daniels echoed.

"Yes. I was recording notes on it, using the voice memo app when Frank arrived. He grabbed the phone from me. As far as I know, it continued recording."

Pete rolled his gorgeous green eyes at me. "And you're just telling us this now?"

"Sorry. It only occurred to me this minute. Apparently my near-death experience threw me off my game, at least for a while. Besides, you know me and technology. We don't always get along too well."

"So where's the phone now?" Pete asked.

"At the bottom of the ravine."

Daniels gave me a funny look. "Huh? How did that happen?"

"Frank put it in the pocket of his vest. It might still be there."

Daniels jumped to his feet and walked to the edge of the ravine. "Hey fellas," he shouted. "Check that body out. Fast. See if there's a cell phone in the vest pocket. If there isn't, look around the ground to see if it may have fallen out."

I wondered if the walkie-talkie device he wore on his shoulder wasn't working.

The coroner's van arrived in a few minutes. And the coroner turned out to be none other than my friend Mike Griswald. My phone was indeed in Frank's vest pocket and – miracle of miracles – he had somehow managed to land on his back. The phone was relatively undamaged, though the battery was low. Daniels plugged it into the charger in his cruiser. We stood there by the open door of the vehicle – me, Pete, Lance, Officer Daniels and Mike – and listened to my fateful, and nearly fatal, conversation with Frank. Daniels nodded several times as he heard Frank's confession to me.

"Well that does it," Daniels announced. "This is all the evidence we'll need to deal with the rest of the Martinez clan." He turned to me. "We will have to hold on to your phone for a bit so we can download this conversation. I'll get it back to you as soon as I can."

"Please tell me you won't need to keep it very long," I said to Daniels. "I will need it to finish my job here."

"Not to worry," he said. "We'll deal with it as quickly as we can. Then we need to locate that gold."

"Any idea how to do that?" I asked.

Daniels smiled. "I think so. This recording is enough to get us a warrant to search the Martinez house. I'm guessing the gold's somewhere in there. And we better move quickly on this, before those folks get wind of what's happening and try to move it somewhere else."

"Speaking of which," Pete said, "I wonder exactly how the Martinez family planned to deal with spending it."

"What do you mean?" Lance asked.

Pete shook his head. "They couldn't exactly walk up to Mrs. Madonna with a handful of gold nuggets and ask to buy her property."

"And it would be equally foolish for them to try to cash it in at the bank," I added. "I guess they would need to sell it somehow."

Pete looked up from his phone and announced, "I just found a website called SellYourGold.com. They say that all you need to do is package your gold up securely and mail it to them. They will send you a check."

Everybody's eyes widened at that. Nobody said a word.

"Okay folks, time to get this show on the road," Daniels said. "We need to get things in motion as fast as possible, then search the Martinez house and arrest the lot of them. Can I offer you a ride back to the ranch? Or the inn?"

Lance turned to me. "You and Pete go with the sheriff. I'll get the horses back to the barn."

"Could you also fill Jess and Clint in on things?" I asked him. "I'm not sure I can deal with that right now."

"Will do. I'll let you know when there's anything new. In the meantime, you should try to relax, maybe get some rest. You've had a bad scare today. It takes time to get over things like this and get back to life as usual."

Lance wasn't wrong about that. It would take some time. The good news was that I was alive. That would have to do for the moment.

Chapter 38

I crashed big time once back in my room. Pete gave me lots of hugs, accompanied by a serious amount of fine whiskey compliments of Clint. I then slept like the dead – or at least the nearly-dead.

The next thing I knew it was mid-morning and an extremely solicitous Pete was luring me awake with breakfast in bed. It was so sweet of him I didn't have the heart to tell him that was something I never really cared for. Bedding down with crumbs wasn't my idea of comfort. Odd that this had never come up before.

Pete had the day all planned out to keep us occupied while waiting to hear from the sheriff. Relaxing by the pool was first on the agenda, followed by the super-deluxe spa treatment. Little by little, I began to feel alive again. And curious as to what was happening with the sheriff.

Clint came by in the afternoon to invite us to a special celebratory dinner. He said the whole crew would be there, including Daniels, who would fill us in of the case. Sounded good to me. Dinner couldn't come soon enough.

* * *

AVENGING MADONNA

Pete and I arrived at the private dining room in the Gold Rush Steak House a little before 6:00. Clint and his wife were at one end of the table, Mrs. Madonna at the other. Jess, Pickens, Rusty, Lance and Brody occupied one side, all duded up in their cowboy best, and in a festive mood. Pete and I joined Mike the coroner and Officer Daniels on the other side. Noticeably absent were Rosa, Alexa and their late brother Frank.

The champagne flowed freely as Clint offered toasts to Lance's prowess as a marksman, my continued existence and the likely end to the rustling problems. Then he said, "I'm going to sit down now and enjoy my shrimp cocktail with the rest of you. While the steaks are cooking, Officer Daniels is going to fill us in on his mighty busy day. Before he does, any of you got something you want to say?"

Pete raised his glass and turned to Lance. "I'd like to thank Lance for saving the life of the woman I love."

I seconded that.

Everybody at the table raised their glasses to Lance.

Lance blushed.

Brody spoke up next. "I'd like to tell Ms. Lynch here how sorry I am for letting her ride out all by herself yesterday. Never should've done that."

"Same here," Lance added.

"And I never should have let that damn Frank know where she was off to," Brody added.

"Not to worry," I told them. "It all ended up just fine."

Nobody spoke for a moment. Then Daniels began, "Guess that means it's my turn."

All eyes and ears turned his way.

"Before I forget," he said, "here's your phone back Ms. Lynch" He passed it down the table to me, then continued, " I'm happy to report that the entire Martinez clan is now in the county jail. They'll be going away for a long time."

This brought on a round of applause.

"Then there's the gold," Daniels said. "We found it in the Martinez house. And not even well hidden. Just sitting in a box on the dining room table like it was waiting to be counted."

"Do we know how much there was?" Clint asked. "Or what it's worth?"

"They're working on that now. It's in a bank vault now, all safe and sound."

Clint spoke up again. "Has anybody figured out who owns it?"

"I did a little research on that today," Pete said. He turned to me and added "while you were at the spa."

The room fell silent, waiting to hear what Pete has learned.

"In general," he said, "the law assumes that items found *in* the land belong to the owner of the land, whereas anything found *on* the land belongs to the true owner of the item in question."

Clint stopped him there. "Does that mean that if the gold hadn't been buried it would belong to the Martinez family?"

"Possibly. If they could prove that it was truly theirs. That's a whole different issue."

"Thank goodness it was buried then," Daniels said. "That saves us all a whole lot of time and trouble."

Pete nodded. "That's right. Even if the Martinez family can prove beyond a doubt that their ancestor buried the gold, there's little they can do about it now because that ancestor sold the land. In fact, the land changed hands more than once over the years. When you purchase something such as land, it includes anything that has been hidden in it."

A look of relief lit up the faces of Mrs. Madonna, Clint and his wife.

It brought a big smile to my face as well.

"I've got a question for you," Jess said to Clint. "What the heck will you do with all that money?"

Clint grinned. "I've actually done some thinking about that – just in case it actually happened."

"And?" Jess asked.

"I'd like to modernize the ranch a bit. I've been looking into some things. There are drone systems available now which could be perfect for monitoring activity out in the hills. We'd be able to spot potential rustlers from far off, and take their pictures as well. That way the guys assigned to the night shift could work from the ranch office. It'd be more efficient, safer, more comfortable."

That brought a nod of approval from everybody at the table.

Clint continued, "On the other hand, I don't want to be too quick to give up the old ways. We'll continue to do head counts, probably more frequently than we have been. I'd also like to start branding again, even if it does reduce the value of the hide. We're raising cattle for the meat to serve here, not for making belts and shoes. It'd be one more thing to help reduce the possibility of rustling."

"And New England Casualty and Indemnity thanks you for that," I told him. "Besides lowering your risk of loss, it would reduce your premiums as well."

My pleasure, Ma'am," Clint said. "Sounds like a win-win."

The steaks arrived, accompanied by twice-baked potatoes and broccoli. Conversation waned as everybody dug in.

Eventually, Mrs. Madonna said, "I've got to tell you, Ms. Lynch, how impressed I am at the way you handled your investigation. Connecting Elena's diary and the gold to the Martinez children was a stroke of genius."

"Having dinner the other night in Morro Bay didn't hurt much either," Lance said, grinning boyishly in my direction.

"What do you mean?" Clint asked.

"Amy and I went there for dinner and ran into the Martinez family. We overheard enough of their conversation to figure out what was going on."

"Dinner?" Pete asked, the color draining from his face.

* * *

Back in the room a while later, Pete broached the subject of dinner with Lance again.

I did my best to roll my eyes at him. "Really, Pete, it was no big deal. Strictly business. And it did help me solve the case."

Pete wasn't buying that. "Strictly business? I'm not so sure about that. I saw the way Lance was looking at you at dinner. It looked more like monkey business to me."

I took his hand. "Don't say that. You know I love you."

"But maybe not quite enough." He shook his head and averted his eyes.

I held my breath and waited for what he'd say next.

"We've been together a few years now," he said. "And it has been wonderful. But it's not enough for me anymore. It isn't going anywhere. I want for us to settle down together and spend the rest of our lives making each other happy. You don't seem interested in that, or ready for it."

I had no answer for that. We sat in silence as I struggled to find something to say.

After what seemed like forever, Pete looked at his watch. "So I guess that's my answer. It's nearly midnight. I'll take an early flight to Boston in the morning. Maybe I should just go to the airport now." He stood, grabbed his overnight bag and headed for the door. At the last minute, he turned to me and said, "See you." Then he was gone.

"See you," I responded, speaking to the closed door.

About the Author

Like her heroine Amy Lynch, P.K. (Paula) Norton spent her career in the insurance industry. When she and her late husband Jack traveled throughout the U.S. and abroad, they entertained themselves by sitting in restaurants discussing interesting ways to kill people. As they plotted all manner of mysterious deaths and mayhem, the world of Amy Lynch was born. Paula's curiosity, passions and varied life adventures are an integral part of her series – interests such as Paris (Paula lived there off and on over the years), archaeology (Paula worked at the archaeological dig in Paris), spies (Paula is a card-carrying member of the Association of Former Intelligence Officers), Key West (Paula's favorite vacation spot), fencing (her husband Jack was an award-winning fencer) and cattle rustling (don't even ask why). Avenging Madonna is the sixth book in the Amy Lynch Investigation series.

When she is not plotting or writing, Paula is, well, plotting and writing. She is a member of Sisters in Crime, the Cape Cod Writers Association and the Association of Rhode Island Authors.

Paula resides in Easton, Massachusetts and Delray Beach, Florida.